BREATHLESS

ELIZABETH KELLY

EK PUBLISHING INC.

BREATHLESS

Who says nice guys can't be bad?

Nice guys are boring. Amanda Martin isn't interested in nice guys and she's spent her entire life chasing after the bad ones. Too bad it's left her broken hearted and convinced true love is a myth. When she meets accountant, Max Westman – a giant of a man and the very epitome of the nice guy – she ignores their unexpected chemistry and insists on friendship only.

But the discovery that Max's nice guy demeanor hides a dirty mind and an even filthier mouth forces Amanda to question her beliefs. If nice guys are so dull, why exactly does she keep imagining a naked Max tied to her bed?

Max wants Amanda as more than just a friend and he's determined to show her that, sometimes, even nice guys are very good at being very bad.

For a FREE Elizabeth Kelly short story, as well as excerpts of upcoming books and contests and giveaways, sign up for Elizabeth's newsletter here

CHAPTER 1

The cliché was right, Amanda mused as she watched her best friend Lucy recite her vows. Brides really did glow on their wedding day. She clutched her bouquet of flowers a little tighter and blinked back the tears as Lucy slid the ring on to Jason's finger.

Jason grinned at Lucy before wiping away the tear sliding down her cheek. As Jason recited his vows, Amanda glanced at the people sitting in the folding chairs. There weren't many. Putting a wedding together in two months didn't leave a lot of time for out-of-town guests to be there, but the people Jason and Lucy loved most were there.

She smiled at Lucy's mom who gave her a quick wink before patting her husband's hand and handing him a tissue. Lucy's dad was weeping shamelessly, and Amanda hid her grin as the man's tear-filled gaze shifted to her. She gave him a subtle thumbs-up and he nodded before wiping at the tears streaming down his face.

She swept her gaze over the other guests. Jason's family were sitting in the front row and the sight of Lenny sitting on Jason's mother's lap almost made her giggle. The large black cat looked supremely pissed off, probably thanks to the white satin bow tied around his neck. She wondered how long it would take before he simply clawed his way free of Rita's lap and bolted for the house.

The breeze picked up a little, blowing a strand of curly blonde hair across her face. It stuck to her lip gloss and she tugged it away as a bit of sand stung her eye. Getting married on the beach was romantic but holy hell did the sand get everywhere. She had no idea how, but she was fairly certain she already had sand in her underwear. She shifted, sinking her bare toes into the warm sand and silently thanking Lucy again for insisting the entire wedding party be barefoot. High heels in the sand would have been a nightmare.

Her stomach did a lazy flip-flop when she caught the stare of the giant sitting in the back row. Like the other guests, he was dressed casually. The beige pants and white dress shirt looked damn good on him, though. He needed a haircut, she thought. His blond hair was almost past his collar. She blushed when he cocked his head and grinned at her. She returned his smile before averting her gaze. Staring at Lucy's coworker, Max, was a bad idea.

Not that bad of an idea.

Yes, it most definitely was. He had already asked her out once and she had turned him down. Her feelings for her ex, Jamie, hadn't changed and it wouldn't do to encourage Max in any way. Even if she did find him smoking hot and had, more than once over the last two months, wondered if his dick was as big as the rest of him.

Jesus, Amanda! You're at your best friend's wedding. Get it together, you sex-starved pervert!

"I now pronounce you husband and wife. You may kiss the bride," the minister said.

The wedding guests cheered as Jason tugged Lucy into

his embrace and kissed her. After a minute or two, Alex, Jason's best friend and best man, nudged him in the back.

"Come up for air, buddy."

Jason released Lucy and grinned at her as she waved her hand in front of her flushed face. Holding Jason's hand, she smiled at their friends and family as the minister cleared his throat.

"May I introduce Mr. and Mrs. Jason Young."

Their family and friends cheered again as Jason and Lucy walked past them. Alex held out his arm and Amanda tucked her hand into the crook of his elbow as they followed Jason and Lucy. Her best friend looked breathtaking in her wedding dress. The bodice of the dress had spaghetti straps and it hugged Lucy's upper body in a classic empire style while the bottom half flowed gracefully over her bottom and hips. It was white satin with only a bit of lace trimming on the hem of the gown and the simple style of it suited both Lucy and their casual beach wedding perfectly.

They were moving past the last row now and she deliberately kept her gaze on Lucy's cascade of long dark hair even though a dismayingly large part of her wanted to glance over at Max. They followed Lucy and Jason to the large canvas tent that had been erected on the beach only a few feet away. She ducked inside and squeezed Alex's arm before letting go and hurrying toward Lucy. She could hear the other guests laughing and talking as they headed to the tent and she wanted to hug Lucy before she was swamped by them.

"Lucy?"

Lucy turned and Amanda wrapped her in a warm hug. "Congratulations, honey. I'm so happy for you."

Lucy beamed at her. "Thank you, Amanda. You know if it hadn't been for you and your intervention and slapping and horrible cookies, this moment might never have happened."

Amanda laughed. "Nope, you and Jason were meant to be. You would have gotten back together eventually. I just hurried the process along with my meddling."

"Well, I for one am extremely grateful for your meddling." Jason grinned at her.

"You're welcome, handsome," she said. "Now, plant one on me before the rest of your guests swarm in here."

She turned her cheek toward him, and he kissed it before taking Lucy's hand again. "I'm starving. When do we eat?"

Lucy whacked him gently on the back. "We still have to say hi to everyone and have photographs. Then you can eat, Mr. Young."

He reached behind her and squeezed her ass as the wedding guests entered the tent. "Whatever you say, Mrs. Young."

"Amanda, what do you say we hit the bar while we're waiting for the two newlyweds to finish talking to their guests?" Alex drawled at her.

"You are required to stay sober until after the pictures are done, Alex," Lucy said.

He saluted her solemnly. "Your wish is my command, Mrs. Young. C'mon, Amanda, let's have a toast to the newlyweds while the wedding guests take bets on whether we end up in bed together tonight."

Amanda laughed and took his offered arm. "Well, when you put it like that – how can I resist?"

"So, are we taking bets on whether Alex and Alex sleep together or not?" Jason asked as he joined Lucy and Amanda at the head table. The party was in full swing with most of the guests dancing in the middle of the tent.

Lucy laughed. "They make a cute couple."

Amanda followed her gaze to where Alex, the best man, was sitting at one of the tables. Lucy and Jason's coworker, Alex, was sitting on his lap and she watched as male Alex cupped her head and pulled her down for a long kiss.

"They're definitely having sex tonight," Jason said. "Although, I thought the best man and maid of honour were supposed to hook up at these things."

He grinned at Amanda as Lucy elbowed him in the stomach. "Jason, behave. But," she glanced meaningfully at Amanda, "if you and Alex started dating, think of how much fun the four of us could have together."

"No, thank you," Amanda said with a grin. "Alex is a nice guy but he's not my type."

Yeah, because he's a nice guy. You only fall in love with the guys who treat you like shit.

She tried to ignore her inner voice. Not that it wasn't right – every guy she'd ever dated had been the quintessential bad boy. She had a type, unfortunately, and she wondered what was wrong with her that made her crave unconditional love from men who weren't capable of it.

"Oh God," Lucy suddenly said. "Dad's breakdancing."

She covered her eyes with her hand as Jason laughed. "That guy is going to have so much sand in his underwear. Lesson one at a beach wedding – never breakdance."

"I can't look – is it over?" Lucy asked as the music ended.

"Yes," Jason replied. "Although it looks like he might show my dad how to breakdance."

The music started again, a song with a slow soft beat and Lucy breathed a sigh of relief. "Thank God, saved by the music."

Jason stood and held out his hand. "Mrs. Young, will you dance with me?"

"I'd love to, Mr. Young," Lucy said.

They joined the other couples dancing in the soft sand and, after a furtive glance around, Amanda slipped her cell phone out of her purse and checked her messages. There was a text from Jamie telling her to have fun at the wedding and she smiled a little. She hadn't told Lucy this, but three weeks ago after a month of Jamie texting and begging for forgiveness, she flew out to New York for the weekend. Jamie paid for the plane ticket and her hotel room and wasn't even upset when she refused to sleep with him. Hell, she hadn't even let him kiss her. She was still pissed about the fact that he had been sleeping with other women even though they were technically no longer dating.

They'd gone to a Broadway show, walked through Central Park, and did a few other touristy things. Since that weekend, he had sent her flowers and daily texts and she was more than a little impressed by his attempts. He had never been like this before, not even when they were dating. She was slowly starting to believe that he actually had changed, that maybe it would be a good idea to date him again.

"May I have this dance?"

She jammed her cell phone back into her purse and smiled at the man standing next to her. "Hi, Max."

"Hello, Amanda. Would you like to dance?"

She hesitated before nodding and taking his hand. A small ribbon of heat unfurled in her belly and she gave him a tentative smile as they joined the other couples. He slid his arm around her waist and held her hand in a loose grip. Her small hand was swallowed by his large one and it sent another ribbon of heat through her. He was so tall she couldn't reach to place her hand on his shoulder, so she settled for resting it on his upper arm.

"How are you?"

"I'm good, thanks. How are you?" she said as he moved her in a slow circle.

"Good. Finally finished unpacking," he replied.

"You must be happy about that."

"I am. It was a very slow and very painful process that I have no one to blame but myself for," he replied with a grin.

She smiled and tried to ignore the shiver down her spine when his big hand gripped her hip a little more firmly. "You're looking lovely, by the way."

"Thanks," she said. "You need a haircut."

"Um, thanks?" he said.

"I'm sorry, I just meant you should make an appointment at the salon," she said then winced. "I mean – you look really lovely too, just long-haired and lovely."

He laughed so loudly that Lucy and Jason who were dancing near them, glanced over. Amanda flushed as Lucy gave her a small grin. She looked hastily away from her best friend. "Sorry, Max."

"It's fine," he said. "I do need a haircut. Maybe I'll make an appointment for next week."

"That sounds good," she said. "You have great hair, it's fun to cut it."

Idiot!

"You know you're not the first hair stylist to tell me that," he said. "It's the little comments like these that I'm going to hold onto when I start going bald."

She laughed and studied his thick hair. "I doubt that's something you have to worry about."

"You haven't met my Uncle Todd. I'm exactly like him – right down to the height and thick hair. I saw pictures of him in the sixties and he had hair down to his waist. Now he's bald as a cue ball, as the saying goes. My aunt says it's just migrated from his head to his back."

Amanda snorted laughter and Max grinned at her. "Someday I'll tell you the story about the time he decided to get my aunt to wax his back. We turned it into a family affair. Ate popcorn and made bets on when he'd start crying and how much wax my aunt would have to use."

"Your poor uncle," Amanda said.

"Poor uncle? He's the one who invited us to watch. He even made my dad record it."

"What? Why?"

He glanced around before leaning down. "Just between us," he said in a low voice, "I'm pretty sure they recorded it so that in the bedroom that night they could watch my uncle writhing in pain. My aunt was only a little over five feet and my uncle towered over her. But when my cousin was a teenager, he came home from school early one day and found my uncle strapped to the bed and my aunt in full Dominatrix mode spanking him with a leather crop."

"No!" Amanda said.

"Hand to God," Max said. "My cousin is still in therapy over it."

She couldn't help laughing, and Max said, "At least now we know why my uncle used to wince every time he sat down."

"So, you're *exactly* like your uncle?" she said teasingly.

"Are you asking me if I like to be spanked?"

"Do you?" She had never spanked a boyfriend and never even had the urge to. So why exactly was this conversation bringing forth an image of Max stretched out in her bed, her small body straddling his while she pinned his arms down and took what she wanted from him? It was a ridiculous illusion – Max was so large he could easily overpower her.

Not if you tied him to your bed. Then you could do whatever you wanted to the big guy.

The thought brought an embarrassing amount of wetness between her thighs.

"Are you offering to spank me?" Max asked.

"If I was, would you let me?" Her voice was breathless and even she could hear the need in it.

She could barely bite back her moan when his big hand dipped lower until it was resting against the top of her ass and he tugged her up against his hard body.

"Butterfly," he said in a low and deliciously sexy voice, "you can do whatever you want to me in your bed."

She shivered all over, her hand tightening in his, and his gaze dropped to her mouth. Her nipples were hardening, a flush was rising up her chest, and her pulse was pounding in her ears. She suddenly wanted Max so much her entire body was aching for him. She waited breathlessly as he bent his large body. He was going to kiss her, and she was going to let him.

"I just realized I haven't danced with the maid of honour yet."

They both jerked in surprise at Lucy's dad's voice. Walter's cheeks were red, and he was weaving slightly. When he held out his hand she pushed away from Max. The song had ended and another one was beginning and without looking at Max, she took Walter's hand. He smiled happily at her as they swayed to the music and she risked a glance over her shoulder. Max was walking back to his table and she frowned at the ridiculous surge of jealousy she felt when one of his co-workers grabbed his arm and steered him back to the dance floor.

Amanda placed the last of the leftover food in the fridge in Lucy and Jason's kitchen before wiping down the counter and throwing some trash in the garbage. It was close to one in the morning and the party had finally wound down. She leaned against the counter for a moment. She should have been tired, she had been up with Lucy at six this morning, but it wasn't weariness coursing through her body. It was lust, pure and simple.

Lust for Max. Go find him.

No, she absolutely couldn't do that. She was in love with Jamie and just because they technically weren't dating, just because it was months since she'd been laid, didn't mean she could fuck someone else. Besides, she was pretty sure she had seen Max leaving as she was carrying the leftovers up to the house.

She pressed a shaking hand on her lower abdomen and willed her damn pussy to behave itself. She was lucky Max had left. The way she was feeling right now, she'd climb him like a damn tree if she saw him.

She heard footsteps behind her and froze when Max's deep voice said, "One more dish of leftovers. Is there room in the fridge?"

Her heart racing, she turned and watched as he opened the fridge and shuffled a few things around before placing the dish in the fridge with the others. He shut the door and she clenched her hands into fists when, instead of leaving, he dropped into a kitchen chair and smiled at her.

"Some party, huh?"

She drifted closer to him, she couldn't help herself, and he gave her a puzzled look.

"Amanda, are you okay? You look flushed."

"Max," she whispered, "I…"

She licked her lips and studied his broad shoulders and

chest as she stopped in front of him. "I really want to kiss you."

If he was surprised, it didn't show on his face. "Go ahead, Butterfly," he said in that low voice that drove her insane with desire.

She stepped between his spread legs and touched his beard with trembling fingers.

"Don't move," she whispered.

He was so tall that even sitting they were face-to-face. She ran her thumb over his bottom lip before pressing her mouth against his. His lips were warm and firm, and she nibbled at his upper lip before slicking her tongue across the bottom one. He groaned and she probed at the seam of his lips with her tongue. He opened them and she slid her tongue into his mouth. He tasted like scotch and she moaned when he sucked on her tongue before pushing his tongue into her mouth. He touched her crooked tooth with the tip of it then flicked his tongue against hers.

He was unbelievably gentle, and she couldn't get enough of his kisses or of the taste of his mouth. She pressed against him and he cupped her ass with those big hands of his and squeezed.

"No moving," she reminded him.

He squeezed her ass again. "This is me not moving. If I were moving, you'd be bent over this table with your dress around your waist and I'd be balls-deep in that hot pussy of yours."

Her mouth dropped open as a tremor of lust so strong it made her legs shake, swept through her. What the hell was going on? Max was one of the good guys and good guys definitely didn't talk like that.

"That was...unexpected," she said.

He grinned at her. "Was it?"

"Yes, you're a nice guy, Max."

"I am."

"Nice guys aren't dirty talkers."

He laughed. "How many nice guys have you dated?"

"Not very many," she admitted.

"Let me guess," he licked her throat with his wet tongue, "you like the bad boys. The ones who charm you, fuck you all night, and are gone before you wake up in the morning."

"I didn't say I had good taste," she said as he nuzzled the base of her throat.

"I'm a nice guy," he said. "I don't play games with a woman and if I'm interested in you," he licked her mouth, "there won't be any doubt. And I'll definitely still be in your bed in the morning."

"Because you're a nice guy," she moaned as he nipped at her earlobe.

"Yes," he breathed into her ear, "and because I love waking a woman up with my tongue in her pussy."

"Fuck!" The word exploded from her mouth and he pressed a soft kiss below her ear.

"That too," he said. "Have any of those bad boys you like so much ever woken you up by sucking on your clit, Butterfly?"

She shook her head, her pelvis aching and her nipples throbbing almost painfully, and he squeezed her ass. "You should consider giving us nice guys a chance. Would you like to know why?"

"Yes," she whispered.

He brushed his mouth against hers, just a gentle caress but it made her entire body tingle. He pulled his head back when she tried to deepen the kiss.

"Because the only thing we care about in bed is making

sure our woman is completely satisfied. Nothing else matters."

She wanted to tell him that the bad boys did that too but, truthfully, they didn't. At least it wasn't her experience. She told herself numerous times that it didn't matter. She was self-aware enough to know that what she craved was the actual chase. It was all about the excitement of 'will he call or won't he', and the delicious thrill that someone like that would want her, not what the actual sex would be like. When they finally did sleep together, more often than not she was left aching and not fully satisfied.

"Invite me into your bed, Butterfly, and you can ride my dick for as long as you need. You can tie me to your bed and have your dirty way with me if that's what you want," he said with a naughty grin.

She thought of the restraints tucked under the top mattress of her bed. A previous lover had given the 'under the bed restraint kit' to her as a birthday gift, although it had technically been for him not her. She hadn't minded being restrained but it wasn't one of her kinks. She had done it more for his pleasure than hers, but he had refused to allow her to use it on him the one time she had suggested it.

An image of Max, his large body stretched out on her bed with the cuffs around his wrists, flooded through her and her pelvis bucked against him uncontrollably. Jesus, the thought of having control over Max like that was setting her on fire with lust.

"Feels like my Butterfly likes that idea," he whispered before capturing her mouth with his.

This time his kiss was hard and insistent. His previous gentleness was gone, and she returned his kisses eagerly, cupping his face and tracing her fingers over his beard as their tongues battled for control.

"Carrie texted me. She dropped Lucy and Jason at the hotel and she's going to take them to the airport in the morning."

Amanda tore away from Max at the sound of Rita's voice, crossing her arms over her chest and giving Jason's parents a nervous smile as they walked into the kitchen.

"Oh!" Rita said. "Oh, I'm so sorry,"

Her face bright red, Amanda shook her head. "No, I…"

She gave both Jason's parents and Max an apologetic look. "I'm sorry. It's very late and I really should get home. I – I'm sorry," she mumbled again before pushing past Jason's dad and escaping the kitchen.

CHAPTER 2

"Amanda, are you sure it's okay if I go?" Gina asked.

Amanda smiled at the receptionist. "Yes. We're closing in less than an hour and I don't have any clients booked."

"Yeah, but I feel bad about leaving you alone," Gina said.

"Don't be silly. It's perfectly safe." Amanda finished sweeping up the hair around her station as Gina shrugged into her jacket.

She continued to hesitate, and Amanda slapped her lightly on the butt. "Go on, honey. It's your birthday for God's sake."

Gina dropped a kiss on her cheek. "Thanks, doll. I owe you." She studied Amanda for a moment. "Hey, are you okay? You've been acting weird all week."

"I'm fine." Amanda smiled at the girl before tugging on her blue locks. "Go and enjoy your birthday. Don't do anything I wouldn't do."

"I feel like that doesn't leave much," Gina said with a grin.

Amanda laughed and pushed her toward the door. "Happy Birthday, honey."

"Thanks, Amanda. I'll see you tomorrow.'

The smile dropped from Amanda's face the moment Gina walked out the door. She rubbed at her temples with the tips of her fingers before crossing behind the desk and dropping into the chair. It was over a week since Lucy had left on her honeymoon and Amanda was counting down the days until she returned. She needed to talk to her about what had happened with Max.

You mean how you made out with him and then left him high and dry in the kitchen? Dick move, Amanda. You could have at least dropped by the office and apologized to him.

She rubbed harder at her temples. Fuck, she was a complete idiot. She had felt guilty and sick to her stomach all week about using Max like that and every time Jamie had texted or called her, she had to stop herself from blurting out what she had done.

You don't need to say anything to that asshole. How many fucking times has he cheated on you? Besides, you're not dating so there was nothing stopping you from kissing Max.

She supposed that was true and, if she was being honest, the guilt she was feeling had less to do with Jamie and more about leading Max on when she had no intention of dating him. She should never have kissed him, and she had spent most of the week trying to figure out why the hell she had lost her mind and practically attacked him in the kitchen.

Because he's hot and sexy and has a filthy mouth that makes you want to let him dick you brainless?

"Oh God," she muttered and dropped her head onto the desk. She needed to apologize to Max.

"Amanda?"

She froze and her heart started to pound rapidly. She was imagining his voice. Obviously. She hadn't heard the bell over the door and –

"Amanda? Are you okay?"

She raised her head and made herself smile. "Hi, Max. I'm fine. Uh, how are you?"

"Good," he said. "I don't have an appointment, but I thought I'd take a chance and see if I could get a haircut tonight."

He ran his hand through his shaggy blond hair, and she suppressed the little shiver that went through her. She should tell him she couldn't, tell him that she had another client, but having an excuse to touch him was too hard to resist.

Lock the door, take him into the back and touch him. Touch him until he's hard and moaning for you to fuck him.

Shut up, brain!

"If this is a bad time, I can make an appointment for another night," Max said.

She shook her head and stood up. "No, not at all. Come to the back and I'll wash your hair."

He shrugged out of his suit jacket and hung it on the coat rack before loosening his tie and unbuttoning the top buttons of his shirt. He followed her into the back room and wedged his body into the chair. She wrapped the cape around him, struggling to fasten it around his thick neck, and he leaned back as she started the water.

He closed his eyes as she massaged his scalp and, when she couldn't stand the silence any longer, she blurted out, "I'm sorry about last week."

"Sorry for kissing me or sorry for running away?" he asked without opening his eyes.

"Both," she said.

"Why are you sorry for kissing me?"

"Because I was feeling a bit lonely that night and I took advantage of our, um, chemistry. I shouldn't have done that."

"I don't see why not," he said. "We're both adults."

She rinsed his thick hair of the shampoo before smoothing conditioner through it. "There's this guy I've been -"

His eyes popped open. "You have a boyfriend?"

"No," she said. "I mean, not really. We used to date, but he moved to New York and we broke up, but we're thinking of trying again. We've been talking a lot and technically we're not dating but there's a good chance that we will be soon."

"Do you love him?"

She jerked, spraying his face with water. "Shit! I'm sorry." She mopped the water from his beard with an extra towel.

"Well, do you?" Max asked.

"Yes," she said. "I'm sorry."

"Being in love is never something to apologize for."

"I shouldn't have kissed you. I took advantage of you and I feel terrible about it."

He shrugged. "Mistakes happen and I'm not upset about it."

"Thank you for being so nice about it," she said. "I don't deserve that."

"You're too hard on yourself," he said. "Besides, us nice guys are used to losing out to the bad boys."

She winced and he said, "I was trying to be funny. I'm really not upset, all right?"

"All right," she said. "I'd like to be friends though. If you would?"

"I would," he said. "I've been finding it difficult to make friends here. Perhaps my personality isn't nearly as charming as my mother has led me to believe?"

She smiled at him. "You're charming, Max. And you'll make an amazing boyfriend to the right girl."

"Maybe I'll get you to text my mom and tell her that. She

worries that I'm going to die old and alone," he said with a grin before relaxing in the chair and closing his eyes again.

"How's that?"

"It looks great. Thanks, Amanda," Max said.

She took off the cape and shook it out as Max stood. He followed her to the reception desk and paid before smiling at her. "I'll wait for you to close up."

"You don't have to," she said. "Really."

"I know. I want to. It's not a good idea for you to be walking to your car alone."

She hurried through the closing duties as he sat in the reception area and scrolled through his phone. They had made a bit of small talk while she cut his hair, but she was feeling awkward and weird despite Max's assurances that he wasn't angry and was open to being friends. She sighed heavily. Why did she always have to fuck up everything?

She shut off the lights and smiled at Max. "I'm ready."

He waited patiently as she set the alarm and locked the door before walking her across the parking lot. He didn't offer her his arm, didn't touch her at all and she told herself it didn't bother her.

"Thanks again, Max. It was good to see you. Maybe we could have coffee sometime?"

"Sure," he said. "I'd like that. Good night, Amanda."

He walked away and she bit back her urge to call his name. What the hell was wrong with her? She sat in her car and turned the key. Nothing happened and she cursed under her breath before trying again.

"C'mon," she muttered before turning the key a third time.

When nothing happened, she popped the hood and climbed out of the car. She checked the connections to the battery, squinting in the dim light, and sighed when they seemed okay. She rubbed at her temples. Her knowledge of cars was limited to how to change a tire and how to jumpstart the battery. She pulled her cell phone from her purse. She would call her dad and ask him to come over and give her a boost.

"Car trouble?"

She screamed and staggered back, gripping her cell phone like a weapon and raising it over her head.

"Whoa, it's me," Max said.

"You scared the hell out of me, Max!"

"Sorry," he said. "I was waiting for you to drive away and when you popped the hood, I figured I'd better check on you. Is your battery dead?"

"Yeah, I think so," she said. "Nothing happens when I turn the key. It's weird though. I had the battery replaced last year.'

"Hold on." He walked to the driver's side and opened the door before turning on the headlights.

"That's a good sign, right?" she said when bright light shone from them.

"Yes and no," he said. "Your battery is fine but that most likely means your starter needs to be replaced."

He tried turning the key before straightening. "Yeah, you're going to need a tow."

"Dammit," she said.

She rubbed at her forehead again and tried to think. She was on a tight budget and she mentally calculated what was left in her bank account. With the cost of the tow and the replacement of the starter, she'd be eating ramen noodles for the rest of the month.

"You don't happen to know how much a repair shop will charge to replace the starter, do you?" she asked Max as he shut off the headlights and closed the door.

"I'm good with cars. Why don't I replace it for you?" Max said. "All you'll need to pay for is the new starter."

"Oh no, that's okay," she said, a little embarrassed. "I didn't mean to make it sound like I couldn't afford to have it fixed."

"Can you?" he asked.

"Probably?"

He laughed. "Let me fix it for you, Amanda. My dad's been a mechanic for forty years and I worked in his shop from the time I was twelve until I went to university. It'll be easy for me to replace it."

She bit at her bottom lip, weighing her options. She didn't want to take advantage of Max again but the thought of eating ramen noodles for the month didn't exactly appeal to her.

"Well, if you're sure you don't mind," she said.

"I don't," he said. "Get it towed back to your place and I'll fix it for you. Do you work tomorrow night?"

"No, I'm done by four."

"Great. Text me your address and I'll come by after work and replace it."

"I'll make you dinner," she said. "It's the least I can do."

"Sure," he said.

"Um, so where does one go to buy a replacement starter?"

He laughed again and she blushed.

"I'll pick up the starter on my way to your place," he said.

"I can pick it up if you tell me where to go and what kind to buy," she said.

"It'll be easier for me to grab it," he said. "I'll give you my cell number – text me your address, okay?"

"Thank you, Max," she said gratefully before adding him as a contact in her phone. "I really appreciate this."

"What are friends for?" he said. "Call the tow truck, I'll wait with you until it gets here."

"You really are the nicest guy," she said.

An odd look crossed his face before he smiled at her. "Thanks."

AMANDA OPENED THE OVEN AND, HOPING FOR THE BEST, lifted the lid of the small roasting pan. The chicken sitting in the middle of it looked like it was cooking correctly. She carefully basted it before leaving the lid off and sliding it back into the oven.

She could feel sweat sliding down her back and it had nothing to do with the heat from the oven. She was a terrible cook and she really shouldn't have offered to make Max dinner.

"You should have offered to take him out for dinner, moron," she grumbled under her breath as she tentatively poked the potatoes that were boiling on the stove.

She had called her mother in a panic this morning for ideas on simple dinner recipes. Once she had convinced her mother that yes, she really was going to try cooking and no, she didn't hate the person she was cooking for, her mother had suggested a roasted chicken and even sent her a recipe for it. It had seemed easy enough and things seemed to be working.

She had her iPad propped up on the counter and she quickly reread the recipe for the garlic mashed potatoes before draining the potatoes and adding the cooked garlic and butter to the pot. She mashed them tentatively, hoping that

Max liked his potatoes a bit on the lumpy side, before checking the clock.

Max had arrived an hour ago, using her bathroom to change from his suit to a t-shirt and pair of jeans before heading outside. She rinsed her hands, put the lid on the potatoes to keep them warm and wandered to the front door.

"Max?" She opened the door, pretending not to notice how well his ass filled out his jeans as he bent over the front of her car, and he looked over his shoulder at her. "Dinner will be ready in about ten minutes."

"Perfect," he said. "I'm almost done."

She went back to the kitchen and finished setting the table before tossing the salad. She checked the clock again and opened the oven. The skin on the chicken had browned nicely and she lifted it from the oven, setting it on top of the stove. She picked up the carving knife and eyed the chicken with some trepidation before brilliance struck her. She'd Youtube how to carve a chicken. How difficult could it be?

She was reaching for the iPad when it rang. There was an incoming video call from Jamie, and she was a little surprised at the thread of irritation she felt. She considered not answering and guilt immediately flooded through her. This was the man she loved. She was not going to ignore his calls because she was cooking a meal for another man.

She propped her iPad back up on the counter and hit the answer button. Jamie's face appeared and he grinned at her.

"Hey, baby. How's my sexy girl?"

"I'm good. How are you?" She lifted the lid of the potatoes and stirred them.

"Are you – are you cooking?" he asked in disbelief.

"Yes," she said.

"Who are you trying to poison?"

"Ha, ha, very funny," she said. "So, what's up?"

"Can't I call my girl just to say hello?"

She smiled at him. "Yes, you just don't normally call to say hello."

"I keep telling you, baby, I'm turning over a new leaf. You're the most important thing to me now and I'm about to be as clingy as you are."

She frowned a little as he laughed. She was making a concentrated effort to be less needy, and to not call him or expect him to be available to talk whenever she wanted. It bugged her that he hadn't even noticed.

"So, why are you cooking?" he asked.

She hesitated. For some odd reason, she didn't want to tell Jamie about Max.

"Maybe I'm trying to improve my skill sets," she teased.

"Baby, you know cooking ain't your thing – being sexy is," Jamie said with a grin. "Speaking of which – why don't you pick up your iPad and go to the bedroom. I've been thinking about you all day and I'm hard as a rock. You can show me how pretty you look when you're touching your -"

"Amanda?" Max wandered into the kitchen. "I'm finished with the car."

"What the fuck?"

Amanda flinched at Jamie's angry shout when it reverberated across the kitchen. She gave Max an apologetic look before glaring at Jamie's face. "Jamie, enough!"

"Who the fuck is this dickhead?" he snapped.

"Max, could you give me a minute?"

"Sure," Max said.

He stepped out into the hallway and Amanda scowled at Jamie. "God, Jamie, could you be -"

"You little whore!" Jamie shouted. "You can't keep your fucking legs shut, can you?"

Her face pale, Amanda took a step back at his fury.

"Jamie, what is wrong with you? Max is a friend. Nothing more."

"Like hell he is, you little slut!" Jamie shouted again. His face was bright red and he leaned closer to the camera. "I should have known that you'd fucking cheat on me."

"I'm not cheating on you," Amanda said. "You're the one who cheated on me, remember?"

"How long are you going to fucking throw that in my face, Amanda? I said I was sorry but that wasn't good enough was it? You have to spread your legs for the first fucking guy who gives you a second look just to get back at me."

"I am not sleeping with Max," Amanda said. "And keep your goddamn voice down."

"Your days of telling me what to do are fucking over! I thought you were different, thought maybe you wouldn't be like every other whore who thinks she can fuck around on me and I won't find out. I put up with your fucking clinging and your neediness and this is how you repay me?"

Jamie was shouting now, spittle flying from his mouth, and fear trickled into her belly despite the fact that he was nowhere near her.

"Calm down," she said.

"Don't tell me to calm the fuck down!" he shouted again. "I brought you to New York, fucking paid for all of it and didn't say a goddamn thing when you wouldn't even let me have a go at your cunt. But you know what? I'm glad you didn't – I don't want anywhere near that stinking, loose-as-hell hole you call a pussy! Who fucking knows what kind of diseases a whore like you has? You're nothing but a selfish, frigid little bitch with sagging tits and a loud mouth who never shuts up. Do you have any idea how many times I wanted to shove my cock in your mouth just to get you to shut the fuck -"

The iPad was plucked from the counter and Amanda watched in silent shock as Max hit the end button before placing it on the table.

"Enough," he said.

"Max -"

"No," he said. "You don't need to listen to the shit he's spewing, Amanda."

The iPad rang. It was shrill and loud in the quiet kitchen and Amanda jumped. She glanced at it and Max shook his head.

"Don't answer it."

"I'm not." She hit the mute button before taking the iPad and throwing it into a kitchen drawer and slamming the drawer shut.

She studied the floor, embarrassed beyond belief. After a moment, Max said, "So, that's the guy you're in love with, huh? He seems great."

She burst into tears and Max muttered a curse before pulling her into his embrace. She leaned her forehead against his chest and cried as he rubbed her back.

"I'm sorry, Amanda. Now is not the time to be a smartass."

"It-it's okay," she sobbed.

"It isn't. I'm sorry."

She probably shouldn't have been clinging to Max the way she was, but the fight with Jamie had left her shaking and feeling sick to her stomach. Jamie had said a lot of cruel things while they were dating but his reaction and the venom in his voice tonight had actually scared her. She'd had no idea he could be that awful and she wondered again what was wrong with her that she'd be attracted to someone like him.

Still feeling shaky and ill, she forced herself to step away from Max. "I'm very sorry."

"You don't have anything to be sorry about."

"He – he's not normally like that," she said. She wasn't sure why she was trying to defend Jamie.

"Isn't he?" Max asked.

"No, well, not usually that bad." She rubbed at the tears on her face.

"He's an asshole, Amanda," Max said.

She stared up at him and then nodded. "Yeah, he is. I'm done with him."

"Good," he said.

She took a shaky breath. "God, I have the worst taste in men. I've been this way my entire life. What's wrong with me, Max?"

"Nothing," he said. "Don't blame yourself for other people's behavior, Amanda. You can't control what they say or think."

"I'm so embarrassed," she said.

"Don't be."

She sighed and grabbed a tissue to blow her nose before washing her hands. She couldn't look Max in the eye. Undoubtedly, he had heard everything Jamie said, and she could feel her cheeks burning. Why had she answered Jamie's call for God's sake?

It's good that you did. Now you finally see who he really is once and for all.

She supposed that was true, but did it have to happen in front of Max?

"We should eat," she said. "The chicken's getting cold. Do you know how to carve a chicken?"

Max nodded and she smiled shakily at him. "If you wouldn't mind carving it, I'll grab the wine, okay?"

"Sure." He squeezed her shoulder briefly. "Amanda, he's a dickhead. Nothing he said was true."

She shrugged. "You don't know me that well, Max. Not everything he said was true but – but truthfully I am kind of clingy and expect a lot from the men I date."

He frowned at her and she shook her head. "It doesn't matter now. I've tried to change and can't so… let's just eat, okay?"

***

"THANK YOU FOR FIXING MY CAR, MAX. I'M SORRY DINNER was so terrible," Amanda said as Max opened the front door and stepped outside.

"It was good," he said.

She barked harsh laughter. The potatoes were lumpy and the chicken so dry it was barely edible. Even the salad seemed limp and tasteless. Not that it mattered to her - she had zero appetite – but she felt terrible for Max.

"It was awful," she said. "I'm a horrible cook. I should have offered to take you out for dinner."

"You're being too hard on yourself," Max said. "I can stay for a while longer, if you'd like."

"No, I'm fine."

"Are you sure? I don't mind. We can watch some TV or talk -"

"No," she said. "I'm fine. Really. I just want to have a hot bath and go to bed."

"Okay," he said. He gave her a worried look. "You can text me anytime you need to, all right?"

"Yeah, sure, thanks," she said wearily. She liked Max but she wished he would leave. She was feeling sick to her stomach and bone-tired and she really needed to cry for about five more hours. She thought again of the horrible things

Jamie had said to her and her stomach rolled with fresh nausea.

"Don't answer his calls, Amanda," Max said. "In fact, block his number."

"Yeah, I will," she said. "Thanks again, Max. I'm sorry the night was such a disaster."

"I told you – you don't need to be sorry." He paused and then leaned down and brushed his lips against her cheek. "Get some rest. Things will be better in the morning."

"You bet," she said. "Good night, Max."

She closed the door and waited until she heard him drive away before bursting into tears.

CHAPTER 3

"Oh, honey," Lucy said before throwing her arm around her and hugging her. "I'm so sorry."

"It's not your fault," Amanda said. She sipped at her coffee as Lenny weaved around her feet.

Lucy and Jason had returned two days ago, and she had forced herself not to immediately call her best friend and cry on her shoulder. In fact, when Lucy had called this morning and told her to get her butt over here and visit while Jason was surfing, she had promised herself she wouldn't even say anything about Jamie. That had lasted for less than five minutes. Lucy had taken one look at her and immediately asked what was wrong. Tears dripping down her face, Amanda blurted out everything. The secret trip to New York, her belief that Jamie had changed, and the dinner with Max that ended so disastrously.

"I was so preoccupied with the wedding that I wasn't even paying any attention to how you were doing," Lucy said. "I suck."

"No, you don't. I purposely hid it from you because I knew you'd tell me that Jamie hadn't changed. I really thought he had – he was so sweet when I was in New York and he called me all the time and…"

She stared into her coffee mug. "I'm such a moron."

"No, you're not. Jamie is really fucking good at making you think he's changed," Lucy said. "Plus, when you love someone it's easy to look past the bad things."

"I don't love him," Amanda said. "Not anymore. The things he said were so horrible, I'll never forgive him for it."

"Then something good has come out of this," Lucy said. "Has he tried to contact you since that night?"

Amanda shrugged. "I don't know. Max suggested I block his number and I did. I don't want anything to do with him anymore. Hell, I don't want anything to do with men in general."

"Don't say that, honey. You just need to find the right guy."

"That's my problem – I have no idea how to find the right guy," Amanda said. "I might be finally finished with Jamie but you and I both know that I'll just find another guy like him. I'm never attracted to the good guys – it's like I fucking crave the drama of a goddamn bad boy."

"You're attracted to Max and he's a good guy," Lucy said.

Amanda shook her head. "I should never have kissed Max in your kitchen. It was a mistake and I feel terrible about it."

"I don't think it was a mistake," Lucy said.

"It was," Amanda insisted. "I'm attracted to Max, but I'll end up hurting him if we dated. Eventually I'll get bored. Remember how much I hurt Rob? He was the only good guy I ever tried dating and look how horrible that turned out. I broke his heart, Lucy, all because I started to get bored."

Lucy frowned at her. "I don't think that's all it was. Rob was a good guy but there were a lot of things that were incompatible between you. Even if you hadn't become bored with him, it would have eventually ended."

"But I still hurt him badly," Amanda said. "I won't do that to Max."

"Well, I think it's a little too early to give up completely on men. Give it some time before you make such a life-changing commitment, okay?" Lucy said with a small grin.

Amanda didn't return her grin. "I mean it, Luce. I'm done with men. I spent all of last night googling how to become a nun. Did you know there's a convent right here in town?"

"Oh God," Lucy said with a laugh. "You are not becoming a nun, Amanda."

"Why not? I think it's the right life choice for me."

"You do remember they don't have sex, right?"

"So?"

"So?" Lucy arched her eyebrow at her. "You love sex. There's no way you're going the rest of your life without it."

"Yeah, well, according to Jamie I suck at it so maybe I'd be doing the men of the world a favour if I became a nun," she said.

"He's an asshole," Lucy reminded her, "with a really small dick and no clue how to make a woman climax. Honestly, woman, I don't even know what you saw in him. He had a bad attitude and was bad in bed."

Amanda shrugged. "I guess I thought I could fix him."

She gave Lucy an anxious look. "I think Jamie was right about one thing – I'm so determined to be in a relationship, so desperate to be loved, that I'll put up with all the shit men pile on me."

"If you think that's true, honey, then maybe it's a good thing that you're taking a break from relationships for a while. You're a strong, capable woman who doesn't need a man to be complete, and some day you'll see that."

The patio door opened and Jason, wearing a wetsuit and with his dark hair wet, walked in. "Hey, Amanda. How's it going?"

"Good," she said. "I see you got lots of sun on your honeymoon."

He laughed. "I did."

Lucy made a noise of exasperation. "Ten days in the Caribbean and Jason comes back with the perfect tan. I, on the other hand, am paler than I was before we left."

Jason laughed again. "I like your pale skin, little Lucy."

He crossed the room and rubbed his wet hair against her face before kissing her. "I'm going to have a quick shower."

He left the room and Amanda stood. "I'd better go."

"Stay for lunch," Lucy said. "I'm making quesadillas and then we're heading to the farmers' market."

"You don't need my sorry ass tagging along with you, Luce."

"Yes, we do," Lucy said. "No arguing with me, Amanda. It won't do you any good to sit around moping at home."

"I think it'll do me a lot of good," Amanda said.

"It won't. Now come on, you can shred the cheese while I get the chicken cooking."

"HEY, LUCY."

"Hello, Max." Lucy smiled at the big man as he sat down next to her in the lunchroom. "How's it going?"

"Can't complain," he said. "You?"

"Good. Now that I'm finally caught up with work. It's only taken a week and a half, but I can finally see the bottom of my inbox," Lucy said.

"I kept meaning to ask you how the honeymoon was but

every time I stuck my head into your office, you were buried in work," Max said.

"It was really great," Lucy replied. "Thanks for coming to the wedding, Max."

"My pleasure," he replied.

He sat silently beside her for a moment, and she gave him a small smile. "What's wrong?"

"Nothing," he said. "I just – I was wondering how Amanda was doing. I assume she told you what happened with Jamie?"

"She did," Lucy said.

"I've texted her a couple times and she keeps saying she's fine but…"

Lucy sighed. "Honestly, I'm a bit worried about her. She goes to work and then goes home and does nothing. I've invited her over every night this week, but she won't come over."

"Jamie said some pretty horrible things," Max said.

"She told me what he said," Lucy said. "He's lucky I don't know where he lives in New York or I'd be flying there and kicking his ass. Thanks for being there for her that night, Max."

"I think she would have been happier if I hadn't been," Max said.

"Maybe, but that's just because she was embarrassed by what happened. I understand that, I do, but this behavior isn't like her, Max. Even when Jamie hurt her in the past, she didn't hide away from the rest of the world."

Max hesitated, "Do you think it would help if I dropped by her place?"

Lucy glanced at him and Max shook his head. "Just as a friend."

"I think it's a good idea," Lucy said thoughtfully. "The

last time I talked to her she was making noise about becoming a nun and I'm a little worried that she's going to run off and join the convent. She could use a friend right now and I think she has this belief that I need to spend all my time with Jason. I'm pretty sure it's part of the reason she keeps refusing to hang out with us."

"I'll check on her tonight on my way home," Max said. "Or is she working?"

Lucy shook her head. "No, she took this weekend off. It's the first time she's had a Friday and Saturday off in forever and I know she's going to spend it holed up in her house the entire time. It would be great if you could convince her to do something fun."

"I'll do my best," Max replied.

"Max? Wh-what are you doing here?" Amanda pulled self-consciously at her ripped and stained t-shirt.

"Lucy told me you had the day off, so I thought I'd drop by and say hello," Max said. "Mind if I come in?"

He shouldered past her before she could reply, his big body taking up most of the narrow hallway, and took off his shoes. "Something smells good."

"Oh, I, uh, ordered a pizza," she said.

"I love pizza," he said.

She didn't say anything, and he hung up his suit jacket. "I'm starving. I skipped lunch today."

"Um, would you like some pizza?"

"I'd love some." He walked into her kitchen and she followed him, watching silently as he lifted the lid of the pizza box.

"Pepperoni and mushroom, my favourite," he said happily. "I don't suppose you have any beer?"

"Bottom of the fridge," she said. She touched her dirty, greasy hair a bit self-consciously as Max opened the fridge and rummaged through it. She hadn't showered this morning, had planned, in fact, on not showering at all this weekend. Despite her talk with Lucy last week, she was wallowing in a sea of self-pity and her weekend plans had consisted of pizza, drinking, and watching *Bridget Jones' Diary* on a continuous loop.

"What were your plans for tonight?" Max said.

"Oh, um, just pizza and movie night," she said.

"Do you mind if I join you?"

"I'm not really great company right now."

"I don't mind," he said. "Besides, if we're watching a movie, we won't be talking, will we?"

"I guess not," she said.

He picked up the pizza box and the two bottles of beer and carried them out of the kitchen. "Grab the plates and the napkins, would you? Which way to the living room?"

"Left," she said. She thought briefly about having a quick shower before dismissing it. She was done with men, what did it matter what she looked or smelled like?

She joined Max in the living room. He had already made himself comfortable on her small couch and she handed him the plates. He slapped down a slice on each plate and twisted the caps off the beer bottles as she sat at the far end of the sofa. Not that it made a difference. Her couch was small, almost a loveseat really, and Max took up more than half of it. Their thighs weren't quite touching, but she was stupidly aware of the heat and bulk of his big body.

"Sorry my couch is so small," she said.

"I'm used to it," he said. "I can sit on the floor though if I'm taking up too much space."

"No, no," she said hastily. "I feel bad because it doesn't look that comfortable."

"I'm good. What movie are we watching?"

"*Bridget Jones' Diary.*"

"Chick flick?"

She nodded and waited for the look of disdain on his face. It didn't appear. Instead, he took a huge bite of pizza and said, "I love chick flicks."

"Like hell you do," she said.

He grinned at her. "Okay, maybe not, but I'm willing to give this Bridget Jones lady a chance. Any sword fights in it?"

"Of course, there isn't," she said. "It's a chick flick, Max."

"*The Princess Bride* has sword fights," he replied.

"*The Princess Bride* is not a chick flick."

It is too." he said with an aghast look on his face. "It's the ultimate chick flick. It's all about true love."

"Don't you mean twue wove?" she asked.

He laughed before taking another bite of pizza. "You know your Princess Bride."

"It's one of my favourites."

"Mine too," he said. "Maybe we should watch it instead."

She shook her head. "It's Bridget Jones night."

"Night? How often have you seen this movie?"

"A few times," she said.

"I'm an accountant – I'm going to need an exact number."

She could feel a small grin starting. "Two hundred and twenty-three."

"Impressive," he said. "If I don't like the movie, will you drop me as a friend?"

"Probably."

"Good to know," he said.

"I LIKED IT," MAX SAID.

"Did you really like it or are you afraid of losing me as a friend?" she asked teasingly.

"No, I really did like it." Max carried the empty pizza box into the kitchen as Amanda followed with the beer bottles. "It was funny."

He threw the pizza box into the recycling bin. "Sorry, I ate all your pizza."

"It's fine."

"It's getting late. I should probably get going," Max said. "Thanks for hanging out with me tonight."

"Thank you," Amanda said. "I really enjoyed your company."

"What are you doing tomorrow?" he asked. "Luce said you had the weekend off."

"Stay in my pajamas all day, eat ice cream and watch *Bridget Jones' Diary* again," she said. "It's what women do when men break their hearts."

"I have a better idea," he said. "I'll pick you up around nine and we'll do what guys do when women break their hearts."

"I'm not going to a strip club."

"What's wrong with strip clubs?"

"Nothing, but I'm not going to one at nine in the morning," Amanda said.

"That's not what we're doing. Although it's good to know you're into strip clubs for our late night adventures."

She tamped down her urge to laugh. "Thanks, but I think I'll stay at home and -"

"Staying at home is boring." He grabbed his jacket and shrugged into it before opening the front door. "I'll pick you up at nine, wear comfortable shoes and clothing."

"Max, I -"

"Bye! See you at nine!" He waved and shut the front door before she could keep arguing.

She sighed and leaned against the door. She didn't want to be around people, she wanted to sit at home and feel sorry for herself.

It'll do you some good to get out of the house. Only, do you think you could shower and wash your hair this time? I know you've sworn off men, but Max is damn hot and with that smell wafting from your body you'll never convince him to sleep with you.

She scowled. She was done with relationships and besides, it would never work with Max.

"PAINTBALL? YOU BROUGHT ME TO PLAY PAINTBALL?" Amanda peered out the window of Max's truck at the large cement building.

He nodded and unbuckled his seatbelt. "It's really great at getting the aggression out."

"I'm not feeling aggressive," she said, "I'm feeling depressed."

"It's good for depression too," he replied. "C'mon, let's go."

"Man, I should have had a second cup of coffee," she grumbled as she hopped out of the truck and slammed the door shut.

"Have you ever played paintball before?" he asked as they entered the building.

"No," she replied. "What are the rules?"

"Shoot me before I shoot you," he advised.

She laughed. "Thanks, that's helpful."

Despite her protests, Max paid for their admission fees and fifteen minutes later she was dressed in a protective vest, facemask, and helmet. Max handed her a pair of goggles and she put them on before striking a pose.

"Do I look dangerous?"

He looked her up and down and a little tingle of heat went through her lower body. She cleared her throat self-consciously as he grinned at her. "Very dangerous."

She scowled poked him in his flat stomach. "You're going down, buddy."

"I do love going down," he said cheerfully, and a hot blush rose in her cheeks.

"Pervert."

"The perviest," he said. "Ready?"

"I guess," she said. "What do I get if I win?"

He shrugged. "We'll do something girlie after this."

"And if I don't win?"

"Strip club it is," he said as he opened the door and led her outside into the bright sunlight.

———

"OKAY, SO YOU KNOW THE PLAN?" THE TEENAGER, HIS FACE muffled by his mask, asked Amanda.

She nodded as she crouched with the three teenagers. They had barely been on the playing field for five minutes when the large group of teenagers had invited them to join their game of 'Capture the Flag'.

"There's only the big guy and Chelsea left on their team," the teenager said excitedly. "Erica and Ben have Chelsea pinned down behind the trees and they'll take her out the minute she tries anything."

He glanced at Amanda. "Remember, make it look real. If Max thinks it's a trap, he won't go for the flag."

"Right," she said. "What happens if he shoots me before you guys ambush him?"

"Sometimes you've got to crack a few eggs to make an omelet," the boy said so seriously that Amanda burst into laughter.

"Shh, Amanda!" The second teenager, she thought his name was Owen, said before looking around. "For a big guy, Max is wicked quiet and fast."

"Sorry," Amanda said.

The three boys held out their fists and she bumped them before they stood and peered around the barrier they were crouched behind.

"Do you see him?"

Owen shook his head. "No, let's go."

MAX WATCHED FROM THE COVER OF THE TREES AS AMANDA fist bumped the three teenagers. Staying low to the ground, they sprinted across the field and disappeared. Amanda crouched behind the barrier, peeking her head up every few seconds to glance at the dark blue flag sticking out of the ground a few feet away.

Max grinned and crept a little closer. Faintly he heard paintball fire and Chelsea's shriek of outrage as she was taken out of the game. He moved quietly forward and reached for a large rock. He threw it over Amanda's head and it landed in front of the barrier with a thud. Amanda popped up from behind the barrier with her paintball gun raised, and he ran up silently behind her and raised his own paintball gun.

"Hello, Butterfly."

She stiffened and muttered a curse before whirling to face him.

"Looks like it's just you, me, and your flag," he said with a grin.

She scowled at him. "You'll never take it alive, Max."

He bellowed laughter. "Have you even hit anyone with a paintball yet?"

"You're only a few feet away. I'll hit you," she said.

He grinned wickedly. "I'm faster, Amanda."

She hesitated before lowering her paintball gun.

"Giving up so easily? It's like you *want* to go to the strip club," he teased.

She flipped him the bird and he laughed again before motioning her to walk toward the flag. "Let's go for a walk, Butterfly. You can watch me take your flag."

She turned and, her hips swaying enticingly, walked slowly toward the flag. He swallowed hard and couldn't resist staring at her ass in her tight jeans as he followed her. God, she had a great ass.

She was at the flag now and she stopped and turned to face him. "Stop looking at my ass, Max."

"I wasn't," he said innocently.

"Like hell you weren't," she said. "Was it worth it?"

"Was what worth it?"

"Staring at my ass instead of checking your surroundings."

There was a soft whistle behind him, and he turned to see her three teammates pop up from behind the barrier.

"Son of a -"

The three teenagers shot him gleefully with paintballs before cheering loudly. He lowered his gun and turned to see Amanda grinning like a maniac at him through her facemask.

"Cold, Amanda. Real cold," he said.

She laughed. "Not my fault you couldn't keep your eyes off my ass long enough to realize it was an ambush."

Her teammates joined her, and she fist bumped with them before grinning at him. "Let's go for a walk, Max. You can watch me take your flag."

"THANKS, MAX."

"You're welcome." He set the cup of tea on the small café table in front of her before gingerly lowering his body onto the chair. It groaned under his bulk and she held her breath, waiting to see if it would simply collapse beneath him.

"I think we're good," he said after a minute.

She smiled at him. "I'll never take being normal-sized for granted again."

He didn't reply and she winced. "God, I'm sorry, Max. That didn't come out right. I didn't mean to make it sound like you're a freak or something."

He laughed. "I know I am."

"You're not," she insisted. "I like the way you look and being tall doesn't make you a freak."

He shrugged and took a sip of his coffee before biting into his scone. Feeling stupid, she quickly changed the subject. "So, what did you think of the butterfly gardens?"

He grinned at her. "Did you take me here because it was the girliest thing you could think of?"

"No," she replied. "I actually really love this place. I've been coming here since I was a kid."

She glanced around the café. It was full of people, the butterfly gardens were a popular tourist attraction, and she was a little surprised they had even managed to find an empty table. She reached under their table and picked up the plastic bag tucked between her feet. "I bought you something."

"You bought me something?"

"Yes. To say thank you for forcing me out of the house. You were right – I needed to get out and have some fun."

She pulled the shirt out of the bag and handed it to him. It was lime green in colour, and he unfolded it and stared at the image of the hot pink Butterfly on the front of it before laughing.

"I love it."

She snickered and took a sip of her tea. "I knew you would. I saw it in the gift shop when you were using the bathroom and it screamed 'Max' to me. I bought three x, it was the largest size they had, so hopefully it fits."

He held it up to his chest. "How's it look with my colouring?"

"Smashing," she said.

They both looked up when the old woman, one shaking hand precariously holding a steaming cup of tea and the other wrapped around her cane, thumped up to their table.

"Mind if I join you?" she asked. "Ain't no other empty spots."

Amanda pulled out the empty chair. "Not at all."

The woman sat with a weary thud and carefully placed her teacup on the table before eyeing Max. "Ain't you a big man. How big are you?"

"I'm 6'7", ma'am," Max said politely as he folded the t-shirt. Amanda took it from him and slipped it neatly into the bag.

"Call me Doris," the old woman said.

"I'm Max and this is Amanda. It's nice to meet you," Max said.

"Nice to meetcha," Doris said before sipping at her tea. "You live here in the city?"

"Yes," Amanda said as Max took another bite of his scone.

"Me too. Been coming to this place since I was in my twenties. Not so many tourists back then." She stared around the café with a hint of disgust on her face. "It's good business for the gardens I suppose, but used to be that my husband and me could walk through the entire gardens and not see a single soul. Just us and the butterflies."

She studied Amanda so intensely that Amanda could feel her cheeks reddening. "You're a short little thing."

"I'm 5'7"," Amanda said a bit defensively. The old woman couldn't have been much taller than 5'3" herself.

Doris ignored her and stared at Max. "I suppose all your girlfriends are short compared to you. Ain't many women around who are over six feet tall, I reckon."

"No, ma'am," Max said.

"Still," Doris eyed Amanda again, "you could have tried to find someone a little taller. It must make things awkward in the bedroom. How exactly do you get things to line up?"

Amanda turned a brilliant shade of red as Max laughed. She glared at him before saying, "Oh, we're not -"

"C'mon now, don't be shy," Doris said, "we're all friends here."

"She rides me a lot," Max said.

Amanda gaped at him as Doris nodded. "That makes sense. My husband was a tall man, not as tall as you but over six feet, and we had to get real creative in the bedroom."

She sipped at her tea as Amanda stared wide-eyed at Max who grinned before taking another drink of his coffee.

"I suppose you figured out that missionary don't work," Doris said to Amanda. "Unless you like having your face smashed into his chest?"

"Um, I…"

"Standing actually works pretty well," Doris said. "O'course, Roger and I used a stool for me to stand on. He was strong but I was quite a bit plumper in my youth, and he didn't have the strength to hold me up the entire time. Although," she eyed first Amanda and then Max, "I don't think that's a problem for you two."

She reached out and squeezed Max's bicep with a trembling hand. "You got lots of muscles, don't you? You work out?"

"Yes, ma'am," Max said.

"Another good one is spooning," Doris continued. "Don't matter what the size difference is in that position."

"Huh," Max said, "that's a good tip. Thanks, Doris."

"You're welcome." She glanced at Amanda. "No need to look so embarrassed, young lady. I may be eighty-two and my Roger may be with the Lord now, but I still remember what it was like to be young and in love."

She finished her tea before standing. "I should go. The bus is leaving for the old folk home in ten minutes and if I'm not on it they'll leave without me. Nice to meet you, Max and Amanda."

"It was nice to meet you, Doris. Take care," Max said as he held out his hand.

Doris shook it before nodding to Amanda. Amanda gave her a weak smile as she limped to the door of the café and headed outside. She glanced at Max, her cheeks still bright red, and said, "Tell me we did not just have a conversation with an eighty-two-year-old woman about sex positions."

"We did," Max said. "And I, for one, thought it was quite helpful. That stool idea is a good one."

He grinned at her and ate the last of his scone as Amanda stared into her cup of tea. Her cheeks were still hot, but it had nothing to do with embarrassment now. Images were flashing through her head – sweet and intoxicating images of sex with Max. She hadn't really thought about the size difference and what that might entail but now she couldn't stop picturing it.

Riding him *would* be the easiest, she thought and a sweet pang of pure lust went through her pelvis as she pictured Max stretched out in her bed while she straddled him. Curiously enough, the restraints were playing a predominant role in this unexpected fantasy, and a shiver went down her spine. What was with her and her obsession with tying Max to her bed?

"Amanda?"

"Yeah?"

"Are you okay?"

"Fine."

He studied her. "You're picturing us having sex, aren't you?"

"No!"

"You totally are."

"I totally am not."

"Of course you're not."

"I'm not," she said. "I was just – I never thought of the size difference before. Did it make things awkward with your previous girlfriends?"

He shrugged. "Sometimes. You make it work. It's like Doris said – you need to be creative."

Tying him to your bed is creative.

Shut up!

She drank the rest of her tea in two large gulps. "Are you

ready to go, Max? I should probably get home and let you enjoy the rest of your day."

"What are your plans?" he said.

"Bridget Jones,"

"Again?"

"Yes. What, uh, are your plans?"

"I didn't have any," he said. "Why don't I make you dinner and watch Bridget Jones with you?"

She laughed. "You don't want to watch it again."

"Sure, I do," he said. "C'mon, Amanda, this is the first time I've actually spent the weekend with someone since I moved here. Don't make me spend my Saturday night at home like a loser. We're having fun, aren't we?"

She hesitated before smiling at him. "We are. But there will be no talking me out of watching Bridget Jones' again. Clear?"

"Crystal," he said.

WHEN SHE SLUMPED AGAINST HIM, MAX CAREFULLY LIFTED his arm. Amanda immediately snuggled closer, wrapping her arm around his waist and resting her head on his broad chest. He stroked her soft blonde hair, and she made a sighing sound.

They were only an hour into the movie when she had started to doze off. He had found it adorable to watch her head bobbing up and down as she struggled to stay awake. He stroked her hair again and took a deep breath. Christ, she smelled as good as ever. He pulled her a little closer to his side, resisting the urge to pull her right into his lap.

He studied the curve of her shoulder before brushing her

hair back and caressing her slender throat. Fuck, her skin was so soft. His groin stirred and he closed his eyes.

Careful, Max. She wants to be just friends, remember?

He remembered. He thought it would be easy to be her friend. He hadn't been kidding when he said he didn't have many friends yet, but it was only one day, and he was already having a hard time keeping his hands to himself. He wanted to touch her, wanted to taste the softness of her mouth again, and it was pure torture to not be allowed.

She's not into nice guys. Even if you could convince her to sleep with you, it would be nothing more than that. Is that what you really want?

No, it definitely wasn't, but already he was at the point where he would take whatever she would give him. God, he was pathetic.

She's giving you her friendship, nothing more.

He sighed and stared blankly at the television as Amanda slept against him.

SHE LIFTED HER HEAD, STARING GROGGILY AROUND AND wiping the drool from her face as the credits rolled on the movie.

"Max? What time is it?"

He glanced at his watch. "Almost ten. You fell asleep halfway through the movie."

"Oh God," she groaned, "I'm so sorry."

"It's fine," he said.

Her gaze dropped to his chest and her eyes widened in horror at the wet mark on his shirt. Oh sweet baby jeebus, she'd drooled on him.

She wiped again at her face, her cheeks turning bright red. "I'm sorry I drooled on you."

He laughed. "Don't worry about it."

She was still curled up against him like a kitten and she was too aware of the heat of his hand on her upper arm and the feel of his hard body against hers. She scrambled off the couch, tripping and nearly falling flat on her face, before shoving her hair out of her face and smiling at him. "I'm really embarrassed. I don't normally fall asleep like that."

"Paintball can be tiring." He stood and patted her arm a bit awkwardly. "I better go. Thanks for hanging out with me today, Amanda."

"Thank you, Max," she said as she followed him to the front door. "I had a lot of fun."

"Me too." He opened the front door and stepped out into the warm night air. "Talk to you later?"

"Yeah," she said. "Drive safe."

"I will. Good night, Amanda."

"Good night, Max."

She started to close the door and then flung it open and stepped out onto the front step. "Hey, Max?"

"Yeah?"

"How do you feel about art?"

He gave her a curious look. "What do you mean?"

"There's an art gallery downtown that's having an exhibition tomorrow of some local artists. I was thinking of going. Would you – do you want to go with me?"

He smiled at her, his even white teeth flashing in the dim light, "I'd love to."

CHAPTER 4

"Hey, Amanda?" Lucy wandered into the kitchen and held up the large blue t-shirt. "Care to explain what this is doing in a gym bag in your guest room? I also found boxers, antiperspirant, and socks the size of my forearm."

Amanda laughed as she pulled the tray of cookies out from the oven. "They belong to Max."

"Max?" Lucy's eyebrows nearly disappeared into her hairline. "You're sleeping with Max?"

"What?" Amanda dropped the tray of cookies on the top of the stove. "Of course I'm not sleeping with Max. You know we're just friends, Luce."

Lucy eyed her carefully. "I know the two of you have been glued at the hip for the last three months and I know the both of you have told me repeatedly that you're just friends, but that was before I found Max's underwear in your spare room."

Amanda laughed again before pouring them both a glass of water and sitting down at the table. "Sometimes he showers here in the morning after the gym. It's crowded at the gym and my place is on his way to work."

Lucy joined her at the table. "He showers here?"

"Sometimes," Amanda said. "It's no big deal. Half the time, I'm still asleep when he's here. He has a quick shower and goes to work."

"Right," Lucy said. "Listen, do I need to be jealous of Max? Because if you tell me that he's your new best friend, I won't hesitate to kick his giant ass."

Amanda popped two of the cookies onto a plate and set them on the table. "You know you'll always be my number one, Lucy."

Lucy laughed. "Just checking. I feel like since I married Jason, we haven't spent very much time together."

Amanda shrugged. "You're a newlywed. I don't want to intrude."

"You wouldn't be," Lucy said. "I'm not the type of person who forgets my friends because I have a husband."

"I know," Amanda said. "It's been fine, really. I've been spending a lot of time with Max so I'm not wallowing in self-pity or anything like that."

"Maybe the four of us could hang out," Lucy said. "Jason and Max are getting along much better at work now. Hell, I think they could actually be friends if they really worked at it."

"Sure," Amanda said. "But it's not double dating or anything like that, Lucy. Okay? We're just friends."

"Why?" Lucy asked.

"What do you mean?"

"Why are you just friends? It's been three months, obviously you two get along like a house on fire, and I know you think he's hot. Why not try dating?"

"Because I'm not ruining my friendship with him. Max is, well, he's really important to me now and if we start dating, I'll ruin everything like I always do."

"You don't ruin everything," Lucy said. "Stop being so hard on yourself."

"I do," Amanda said. "Even now, I have to stop myself sometimes from being too – too clingy with Max and we're just friends. Could you imagine how I would be if we were dating? I'd start expecting him to be there for me for every single little thing, like I always do with my boyfriends. Before long Max would hate me for it."

"Here's the thing, Amanda. Those guys you dated before? Your bad boys? They only found it annoying because they weren't boyfriend material. You're not clingy or demanding – you just have really bad taste in men. Max is a good guy, and I don't think it would bother him in the least."

"He is a good guy," Amanda said. "He's sweet and caring and – and *nice*. I don't date nice guys, remember?"

"Maybe you should," Lucy said.

"I'll end up hurting him," Amanda said.

"Don't take this the wrong way, honey, but you sound like a broken record," Lucy said.

Amanda scowled at her. "I'm not going to date Max. Period."

Lucy cocked her head at her. "So, you're telling me there's no part of you that finds Max attractive? You don't ever imagine what it would be like to sex that big guy up?"

"Lucy!"

"What? His socks are the size of my forearm. Like you haven't wondered about the size of his dick."

Amanda burst into laughter. "I don't think about Max's dick, Lucy."

"Liar," Lucy said.

"Fine. Maybe I think about it occasionally, but -"

"Only every once in a while, or every time you masturbate?" Lucy asked.

"Lucy!"

"You think he's good looking, admit it," Lucy said. "When you came by the office to have lunch with him the other day, I saw you checking out his ass."

"He has a nice ass," Amanda admitted.

"That he does," Lucy said. Her cell phone rang, and she pulled it from her purse. "It's Jason, give me a second."

As Lucy answered her phone, Amanda stared out the kitchen window. Her pulse was racing, and she hoped her cheeks weren't flushed. Lucy was closer to the truth than she knew. Amanda drank her glass of water in three large gulps before pouring herself some more. She did think about Max's dick, thought about it way more than she should, and it was only getting worse with each passing day.

Hell, she even dreamed about him now. Dreamed about having him in her bed, his low voice whispering in her ear as she rode him to her climax. She would wake up from those dreams, wet and aching and full of need, and would almost always masturbate. It didn't help - the orgasms she gave herself never seemed to fully satisfy that ache in her pelvis.

She shivered all over as her fingers clenched around her water glass. She couldn't sleep with Max, no matter how much she wanted him. Besides, his attraction to her was over. He was always the perfect gentleman and she never caught him checking out her tits and ass. She sighed inwardly. She thought she was being subtle about checking him out but if Lucy was seeing it…

"Amanda?"

She glanced up to see Lucy staring at her.

"Everything okay?"

"Yes. Eat a cookie."

She pushed the plate of cookies toward Lucy before taking one for herself. She bit into it, grimacing at its dry and tasteless texture and spit it out into a napkin. "On second thought, don't eat the cookie."

Lucy laughed and set the cookie back on the plate. "Thanks for the warning."

"I KNOW WHAT YOUR EVIL PLAN IS, YOU KNOW."

Amanda placed the bowl of popcorn on the coffee table before sitting next to Max. "What are you talking about?"

"You think if you make me watch Bridget Jones every weekend that eventually I'll cave and watch the sequel. It's never going to happen," Max said.

"I don't make you watch it *every* weekend. We watched *The Princess Bride* last weekend," she said before wincing and rubbing at her thighs. "God, Max, I really don't know how I let you talk me into joining the gym. It's been two weeks and my thigh muscles are still killing me. Shouldn't I be all buff and pain free by now?"

Max laughed and patted her aching thigh. "It takes longer than two weeks. Besides, the benefits outweigh the pain. You're sleeping better at night, aren't you?"

"Yes. Maybe a little too better. I can barely stay awake through the movie now," she said with a grin.

"Maybe if we watched something other than Bridget Jones, you wouldn't fall asleep."

She stuck her tongue out at him before leaning against him. "Start the movie, Mister Smarty-Pants."

SHE WOKE AS THE CREDITS WERE ROLLING. SHE CRANED HER head to stare at Max, smiling a little when she saw that he had fallen asleep as well. His arm was around her and she was snuggled in like a kitten against his warm body. She studied him for a moment before running her hand across his broad chest. God, he had an amazing body.

I bet it looks even better naked.

Yes, probably. She would never admit this to Lucy but there was more than once when Max was showering at her place that she had deliberated accidentally walking in on him. Considering that Max was rapidly becoming one of her best friends, the amount of time she spent fantasizing about his naked body was ridiculously inappropriate. She reached up and touched his beard, stroking it with her fingertips before running her thumb across his full bottom lip.

He muttered something in his sleep before shifting on the couch and she guiltily snatched away her hand. She really shouldn't be groping Max in his sleep. In fact, it was best to move before she really did something stupid. She tried to wiggle free of his arm, making a small squeak of protest when his arm immediately tightened. She was trapped against him and she paused for a moment before rubbing his chest again.

"Max? Wake up, big guy."

He didn't move and she patted his chest. "Max? Time to wake up. The movie's over."

He snorted and pulled her even closer. She winced at the pressure on her ribs and gave him a harder pat. "Max, I can't breathe."

His eyelids fluttered and he stared sleepily at her.

"Hey," she said. "Guess I'm not the only one who falls asleep during movies."

"Hello, Butterfly," he said in an adorably sleepy voice. She squeaked in surprise when he lifted her onto his lap.

"Max -"

She was cut off by the firm pressure of his lips against hers. His big hand cupped her face, holding her steady, as he licked at her mouth. With a small moan, she parted her lips, and he flicked his tongue against her crooked tooth before licking at her tongue.

This was wrong - really, really, wrong – and the right thing to do would be to pull away. Max was half-asleep and had no idea what he was doing. She needed to move away and wake him up. She would do exactly that – as soon as she had kissed him for just a few more minutes. She pressed herself closer, sucking on his tongue as he rubbed her back and curled his fingers into her long hair.

"You smell so good," he muttered. He buried his face in her neck and inhaled before licking her throat.

She gasped with pleasure, her hands digging into his shoulders as she ground her ass against the large bulge pressing against her. He groaned and turned her on his lap until she was straddling him. He held her ass and she rubbed her pussy against his erection. She moaned, feverishly wishing that neither of them were wearing jeans. Her panties were soaked through already and she was aching to be filled with Max's cock.

He cupped her breast through her shirt, squeezing it as her nipple rose into a stiff peak against his palm. He kissed her again, slanting his mouth over hers and exploring every inch of her mouth as she rubbed her body against him. He slipped his hand under her shirt and traced his fingers over her abdomen, circling her navel with his index finger.

"Max, please," she said. "Please touch me."

He stiffened against her and she stared at him in confusion when he pulled his hand out from under her shirt. He blinked rapidly before staring around the living room.

"Fuck," he muttered. He lifted her off of him and sat her

on the couch before standing. The bulge in his jeans was mouth-wateringly large. She had to clench her hands into tight fists to stop from simply clawing at the buttons and yanking down his jeans.

Max ran his hand through his hair. "Jesus, I'm sorry, Amanda. I must have fallen asleep. I thought I was dreaming and I... I'm really sorry."

"It's fine," she said shakily. Her pelvis was throbbing, and her entire body felt like it was on fire with lust for Max.

"I don't usually grope women in my sleep, I swear," Max said.

She made herself smile at him. "I know."

He gave her a searching look before grabbing his cell phone from the table. "It's getting late. I should go."

She stood and followed him on trembling legs to the front door. As he opened it, she lurched forward and grabbed his arm. "Max!"

He looked over his shoulder at her, his eyes dropping to her small breasts for a moment before he stared at the floor.

"We're still friends, right?" she said.

He nodded and gave her a more natural smile. "Of course we are. I'll text you tomorrow, okay?"

"Okay."

The door shut behind him and Amanda bolted for the kitchen. She grabbed her cell phone and called Lucy.

"Hey, gorgeous, what's up?"

"Did I wake you? I know it's late," Amanda said.

"Nope. Jason and I just finished taking a moonlight stroll on the beach. It was very romantic – well, if you don't mind the smell of rotting fish. Let me tell you, sometimes living on the beach isn't all it's cracked up to be."

She heard Jason's low voice murmuring in the background and Lucy laughed. "Rotten fish is not an aphrodisiac, Jason Young."

"You sound busy, I'll let you go," Amanda said.

"What? No, don't. I have time to talk. What's up?"

"I – I kissed Max tonight."

"What?"

"Well, technically he kissed me, but he was sleeping and didn't really mean it. I should have stopped it, but I didn't, and now I think I fucked up our friendship and why the hell didn't I stop him when he was sleep-kissing me, Lucy!"

She ran out of breath and there were a few seconds of silence before Lucy said, "Max sleep-kissed you?"

Amanda groaned and sank into the kitchen chair. "Sort of. We were watching a movie and we both fell asleep on the couch. I woke up first and I, well, I might have touched him a little bit but just like innocent touching."

"How innocent?" Lucy asked. "Was there penis grabbing?"

"God, no, Lucy! I touched his chest and his face," Amanda said. "Anyway, I knew I was making a mistake, so I tried to move away from him. But he had his arm around me and he's so strong I couldn't get free. So, then I tried waking him up and he kind of woke up but then hauled me into his lap and started kissing me and – and touching me."

"Wow," Lucy said. "Did you like it?"

"I – what?'

"Did you like kissing him?"

"Yeah," Amanda said. "I liked it too fucking much. I would have screwed him right there on the couch if…"

"If what?" Lucy asked.

"Max stopped it. He said he thought he was dreaming and when he woke up fully, he couldn't get away from me fast enough. The look on his face, Luce – ugh, I wanted to die of shame."

"Hmm, that doesn't sound promising."

"He – he used to be attracted to me, I used to catch him staring at my ass or my boobs but the last couple of months he's changed. We spend tons of time together and he doesn't do or say anything that isn't just, well, friendly. He kissed me tonight because he was half-asleep."

"That's good, isn't it?" Lucy said. "You want to be just friends with him."

"Yes, that's good," Amanda said.

"Amanda…"

Amanda swore under her breath. "I'm so messed up, Lucy. I love being his friend and I don't want to lose that, but I also want to fuck his goddamn brains out. I shouldn't even be attracted to him."

"Why not? Max is hot as hell," Lucy said.

There was a disgruntled holler in the background and Lucy laughed. "Uh oh, Jason heard me say that. I'm in for a spanking tonight for sure."

Amanda snorted laughter. "Nice."

"Back to Max and why you shouldn't be attracted to him," Lucy said. "I don't get why you think that."

"Because he's nice," Amanda said.

"If I hear you talk about Max being nice one more time, I'm coming over there and kicking your ass," Lucy said. "There's nothing wrong with a nice guy."

Lucy sounded cheerful enough, but Amanda could hear the underlying annoyance in her voice. She sighed. "For most women, no. But you know how I am."

"No, I know how you *think* you are. Honestly, Amanda, do you know how many women would kill to have a guy like Max? I'm surprised he hasn't already been snatched up. He's a real catch, and I'm starting to think I need to have one of your interventions to make you see that."

"I know how awesome he is," Amanda said. "I spend every weekend with him for God's sake. But I'm not going to hurt him and right now I don't trust that I won't hurt him if we started dating. Besides, I'm done with relationships, remember? I suck at them."

"Do you hear that noise?" Lucy asked.

Amanda listened carefully. "No, what noise?"

"It's the sound of a dead horse being beaten," Lucy said. "Amanda, I love you and I'm only going to tell you this one more time – you do not suck at relationships, you suck at picking out good men. Max is a good man. Take a chance, honey."

"It's too late," Amanda said. "We're in the friend zone now."

"Maybe, maybe not," Lucy said. "I can talk to Max at work on Monday – casually ask him how he feels about you."

"God, no," Amanda said. "He'll know I put you up to it. Listen, I'm going to let you go. It's getting late and I know you've got a spanking to get to."

Lucy laughed. "That I do, my friend. That I do."

———

TUESDAY NIGHT, AMANDA TOSSED HER PURSE ON THE COFFEE table and collapsed on the couch with a soft groan. The salon was stupidly busy today and her period had started yesterday and she was cramping like a bitch. She rubbed her lower abdomen, wincing as dull pain throbbed through her pelvis, before standing and heading to the bathroom. She reached under the sink and cursed vehemently when she discovered the empty tampon box. She headed upstairs to the master bathroom for her emergency box. Tears dripped down her face when it was empty as well.

"Keep it together, Amanda", she muttered as her stomach throbbed. It was only a ten minute drive to the nearest grocery store but she really wanted to put on her pajamas and crawl into bed. Rubbing at her forehead - headaches were always a side effect of her cycle – she slipped into her shoes, grabbed her purse, and walked wearily to the front door before yanking it open.

She screamed and staggered back. Max was standing on her doorstep and he reached out and caught her as she tripped over her own feet.

"Sorry, Amanda. I didn't mean to scare you."

"Max, wh-what are you doing here?" She asked as he released her and shoved his hands into his pockets.

"I thought I would drop by and see if you wanted to go for coffee. I feel like I owe you a better apology for Saturday night."

"You don't," she said. "Really, you don't."

He took a careful look at her. "Are you okay?"

She nodded. "Yes, I'm, um, not feeling well today."

"Do you have the flu?" He reached out and pressed his hand against her forehead. "You feel warm. Were you going to the walk-in clinic?"

"No, I don't have the flu," she said. "I'm fine, Max."

"You don't look fine. Where were you going?"

"I need to pick up a few things at the grocery store," she said.

"Can it wait? You're really pale and it looks like you're going to pass out. Did you eat supper?" Max said.

She smiled distractedly at him. Her pelvis was really throbbing now, and her headache was making her feel nauseous.

"Amanda? Did you eat?"

She shook her head. "No. I'm sorry, Max, I really need to run out and pick up some stuff. Can I text you later?"

"Why don't I grab the stuff for you? Make me a list and you can climb into bed and rest," Max said.

"Oh no, that's okay."

"I insist," he said. "What do you need at the grocery store?"

"Nothing you want to pick up, trust me."

"Amanda," he said, "you look like you're going to faint. Tell me what you need, and I'll get it."

Another cramp went through her belly and she winced and grabbed her abdomen as Max gave her an alarmed look. "Amanda, what -"

"It's my period," she said. "I have my goddamn period and it's really bad and I'm completely out of tampons. That's what I need at the grocery store. Okay, Max? Jesus."

She rubbed at her forehead again and stared dully at the floor. She was being a complete bitch to Max, and she was dangerously close to bursting into tears.

"What brand?"

She looked up in surprise as Max said again, "What brand, Amanda?"

"I'm not making you buy tampons for me," she said. "That's asking too much and I'm not embarrassing you like that."

He rolled his eyes. "Buying tampons is not embarrassing for me. C'mon, let's get you into bed."

He took her arm and led her up the stairs to her bedroom. He sat her on the bed and took off her shoes before handing her the pajamas that were at the end of the bed and disappearing into the bathroom. She changed into her pajamas and climbed into bed as Max yelled, "You decent?"

"Yes," she replied as she pulled up the covers.

He came out of the bathroom with a glass of water and a bottle of Advil. "Here, take two of these. It will help with the cramps."

She smiled at him and swallowed the pills obediently. "Thanks, Max."

"You're welcome." He pulled her cell phone out of her purse and handed it to her. "Text me the brand of tampons and anything else you need, okay?"

She hesitated and he gave her a quick peck on the forehead. "I really don't mind. I promise."

She winced as another cramp rippled through her and Max pressed her back into the bed. "I'll be back in half an hour, okay?"

She nodded and caught his hand. "Max, I – thank you so much. I'm sorry I was a bitch earlier."

"You weren't. I'll be back soon."

She sat up when she heard the front door open. It had been closer to forty minutes and she slid out of bed as Max climbed the stairs and walked into her bedroom. He rummaged through the plastic bag and pulled out the box of tampons.

"Thank you, Max," she said before hurrying into the bathroom. When she emerged a few minutes later, Max was plugging in a heating pad and there was a delicious smell drifting from a paper bag on the dresser.

"Is the Advil kicking in yet?" he asked.

"A little," she said. Her pelvis was still throbbing, but she thought her headache was a little better. "What smells so good?"

"Soup," he said as he piled the pillows against the head-board and pulled back the covers. "Climb back into bed."

She climbed in, smiling a little when he rearranged the pillows behind her back before placing the heating pad across her lower abdomen.

"I checked for a heating pad in the bathroom earlier and didn't see one, so I went ahead and picked up one," he said as he patted her bare thigh before pulling up the covers. "It'll help with the cramping."

She smiled tiredly at him. "You think of everything, don't you?"

He shrugged before crossing to the dresser and pulling two containers of soup, plastic spoons and two bottles of water out of the bag. He brought them to the bed and made himself comfortable on the other side of the bed before opening her container of soup and passing it to her.

"Can you try and eat a little?" he said. "It'll help with your headache."

"How did you know I have a headache?"

He shrugged again. "You always get headaches when you have your period."

"How do you know that?"

"I'm observant," he said.

"Yeah, but you know when my cycle is?" she said in disbelief.

He laughed. "Well, I don't know the exact date you get your period, but you're always pale and tend to have headaches when it happens so…"

He grinned at her. "Plus, you get kind of cranky."

She gave him a mock scowl. "You'd be cranky too if you had a uterus that was contracting."

"Actually, I'd probably be on the floor in the fetal position and screaming for a merciful death," he said before opening his own container of soup and eating a mouthful.

She laughed and took a small sip of her soup. "It's not that bad."

"It looks pretty bad."

"Well, it's not great," she admitted. "Honestly, the cramping is awful, but Advil usually helps make it tolerable at least. The parts I hate are the mood swings and the random bouts of crying. It's such a cliché but I totally act like men think women act when they have their period. It drives me crazy."

"You seem okay to me," he said.

"You didn't see me crying when I realized I was out of tampons," she said. "Thanks again for picking them up for me, Max. I promise to do something equally embarrassing for you."

"I told you – it's not embarrassing," he said.

She stared at the steam rising from her soup. Once, while at a party with Jamie, her period had come early. She'd told Jamie, ignoring his grimace of disgust, but when he realized that she needed to go home, he was beyond pissed at her. She closed her eyes, remembering the huge fight they'd had once they were at her house. He accused her of starting her period early on purpose because she didn't want to be at the party. They screamed at each other for half an hour before he stormed out of the house. He didn't call her for three days but when he finally returned, not quite apologizing but acting sheepish, she forgave him like she always did.

"Amanda? You okay?"

She smiled at Max. "Yes. Thank you for the soup. It's very good."

"You're welcome," he said.

They finished their soup in silence. He frowned when she

only ate half of hers but didn't say anything, and he took the containers to the kitchen before returning to her bedroom.

"I guess I should probably go and let you get some sleep," he said.

She smiled tentatively at him. "If you don't have other plans, why don't you stay? I wouldn't mind the company."

"Sure," he said. He relaxed on the bed beside her, stretching out on his back and tucking his hands under his head as she curled up on her side beside him. She kept the heating pad pressed against her abdomen and smiled at the way his feet and calves hung over the end of the bed.

"Sorry, my bed is way too small for you."

"Most beds are," he said. "I had mine custom made. It's huge and pretty much fills up the entire bedroom. I had to toss my dresser when I moved into my place here – there wasn't enough room for it and the bed."

She rubbed at her temples and he frowned. "Maybe I should go. I don't think you're in the mood for visiting."

"I don't want you to go. I don't feel much like talking but tell me about your day."

She closed her eyes and rested her forehead against Max's ribcage. After a moment, he slid his arm around her and she curled up closer to him, resting her head on his chest and draping her arm across his flat stomach. He rubbed her lower back, and she made a soft groan of happiness. "That feels really good."

He continued to rub her back as he told her about his day. The sound of his low voice and the steady thump of his heartbeat beneath her cheek soon lulled her into sleep.

She woke a little after midnight. The room was dark, but Max's solid warmth was still against her and she could hear his soft snoring. She smiled and slid out of the bed before using the bathroom and brushing her teeth. She crept back into the bedroom and eased into the bed again. She probably should do the right thing and wake up Max, but he was sleeping soundly and she liked the feel of his body next to hers. She curled up on her left side – there was a very large part of her that wanted to snuggle up to Max again, but she curbed it fiercely – and tucked her hand under her pillow. Max shifted beside her and a current of disappointment went through her. He would wake up and then he would leave.

Her eyes widened when instead of leaving, Max turned on his side and spooned her. His big hand cupped her breast and he nuzzled the back of her neck before muttering, "Night, Butterfly."

"Good night, Max," she whispered.

"Wake up, Amanda."

She squinted blearily at Max. He was sitting next to her on the bed, and she struggled into a sitting position. She patted self-consciously at her hair, wondering how bad her bedhead was, as Max gave her an apologetic smile.

"I'm sorry. I fell asleep in your bed."

"That's okay," she said. "What time is it?"

"A little after five. I'd better go. I want to go to the gym before work this morning. Are you feeling better?"

She nodded and he patted her arm. "Good, I'm glad. I'll text you later, okay?"

"Okay," she said before yawning.

He grinned and tugged on a lock of her hair. "Thanks for letting me crash at your place. I hope my snoring didn't keep you awake."

"It didn't," she said. "Thank you again for everything last night. It was really nice of you."

A small grimace crossed his face before he smiled at her and stood. "Bye, Amanda."

"Bye, Max. Have a good day, okay?"

"You too."

He left the bedroom and she relaxed in the bed, staring up at the ceiling as she heard the quiet rumble of Max's truck. She was tempted to try to go back to sleep before she sat up and threw back the covers. She would have a hot bath and not think about how nice it was to have Max in her bed and how much she wanted him in her bed again.

CHAPTER 5

Amanda washed her hands and dried them before leaving the bathroom. She smiled at Bethany, who was washing a client's hair in the back room, and headed back to her station. She had one more appointment and then she was meeting Max for dinner. He'd stopped at her place on Wednesday and Thursday after work to see how she was feeling and if she needed anything. They ate dinner together both nights but on Friday afternoon he flew to his parents' place. He didn't come back until Monday night and she was a little alarmed at how much she missed their weekend ritual. She spent Saturday night bored and restless and while she went to the gym Sunday morning, it wasn't the same without Max there to encourage her and give her tips on the machines. She offered to pick him up at the airport Monday night, but his flight was getting in late and he insisted he could take a cab.

She couldn't resist texting him this morning and asking him to have dinner with her tonight. She knew he would be tired from his trip and his late night, but she was thrilled when he had texted immediately and agreed to dinner.

A smile crossed her face and she slowed to a stop and checked her hair in the mirror at Bethany's station. She hadn't asked Bethany to curl it for any specific reason. It was slow at the salon this afternoon and they were both bored, that's all. She certainly hadn't curled it because she was having dinner with Max tonight.

"Gosh, Mr. Westman, you really are the biggest man I've ever met."

Gina's girlish giggle made her head snap up and she watched as the receptionist reached out and stroked Max's arm as he leaned against the desk.

"How tall are you, Mr. Westman?"

"I'm 6'7" and call me Max."

"Max," Gina said before squeezing Max's arm again.

Amanda hurried forward. "Max? What are you doing here?"

"We're having dinner, remember?" he said.

"Yes," she said, "but I have one more appointment."

"Sorry, I know I'm early," he said. "I'll head over to Starbucks and -"

"Don't be silly," Gina said. "We have coffee here. Sit down and I'll bring you a cup, Max. Go on now. I can keep you company while you're waiting for Amanda."

"Sure," Max said. He grinned at Amanda. "Your hair looks cute."

"Uh, thanks," she said.

Cute? It looks cute?

She ignored her outraged inner voice and followed Gina to the coffee machine.

"Holy shit, Amanda. Tell me you're not dating him. Please," Gina said in an excited whisper.

"I'm," for a moment she was tempted to lie, and she bit it back fiercely. "I'm not dating Max, we're just friends."

"Sweet," Gina crowed. "You don't mind if I work my magic on him, do you?"

"Oh, uh, I don't really think Max is your type, Gina," Amanda said.

"Why not?" Gina asked.

"Well, he's an accountant and, um, a little on the boring side. You don't like boring."

"For him, I'd make an exception," Gina said with a grin. "Besides, he doesn't look boring, and he was kind of flirting with me while you were in the bathroom."

"He was?" Jealousy streaked through her stomach.

Gina nodded. "Yes."

The bell over the door rang and Gina waved at the woman standing by the desk. "Hello, Mrs. Bell. Amanda will be right with you."

"Gina, Max isn't really the flirting type, are you sure that he was flirting with you?"

"I'm sure," Gina said. "Go on and help Mrs. Bell, gorgeous girl. I'll keep Max entertained."

She grinned and winked at her and Amanda forced a stiff smile before walking toward her client She and Max were just friends – it didn't bother her that he was flirting with Gina. It didn't bother her at all.

"What's wrong, Amanda?"

"There's nothing wrong."

"Bullshit," Max said. "You haven't eaten anything, and you've barely said two words tonight. Did you have a bad day at work?"

"Something like that," she muttered.

She pushed the food around her plate as Max stared

silently at her. Finally, he said, "Why don't you tell me what happened?"

"Do you like Gina?"

"I'm sorry?"

"Gina, the receptionist at the salon. Do you like her?"

"I just met her tonight. I barely know her."

"She said you were flirting with her." She hated the accusing tone in her voice.

"I'm a natural flirt, what can I say?" He laughed.

"She's not your type, Max."

"How do you know what my type is?" he asked with a grin.

"She isn't into boring guys and -"

"So now I'm boring?"

"What? No, that isn't what I meant," she said. "I mean that she likes bad boys and you're -"

"Yeah, I know. Give it a rest, would you, Amanda? I'm well aware that you think I'm nice and boring."

He was staring angrily at her and panic erupted in her belly. For the first time since she'd met him, his easy-going nature had disappeared. She reached out and grabbed his hand. "No, Max, I'm sorry. I didn't mean it that way, I swear. It's just – Gina does like the bad boys and she'll break your heart if you -"

"If I what, Amanda? If I date her? If I sleep with her? I don't need you worrying about my love life. Besides, maybe Gina sees something in me that you don't. Did you ever think of that?"

"Max, I -"

"I get that my *niceness* is about as attractive to you as a wart but, believe it or not, some women aren't disgusted by it."

"I'm not disgusted by it," she said. "Max, I just don't want you to get hurt."

He yanked his hand free. "Forget it, Amanda. Listen, I hate to bail in the middle of dinner, but I've had a rotten day myself and I'm tired and I have a bad headache. Do you mind if I call it a night?"

He pulled some bills from his wallet and set them down on the table as she blinked back the tears. "Please don't leave. I'm sorry. I didn't mean to be so thoughtless. Tell me why your day was so awful."

"I'd rather just go home," he said. "I'll text you later, okay?"

She nodded, the lump in her throat nearly choking her as he shoved his wallet into his pocket and left the restaurant. She stared at her uneaten plate of food, blinking back the tears as her throat ached and burned.

"WE'RE LEAVING IN FIVE MINUTES, LUCE," JASON CALLED through the door.

"Almost finished, honey." Lucy added more gloss to her lips before smiling at Amanda. "How do I look?"

"Gorgeous," Amanda said. She was standing in Lucy and Jason's bedroom and she petted Lenny absentmindedly as he weaved around her feet.

"Thanks," Lucy said. She suddenly grimaced and rubbed at her stomach.

"What's wrong?" Amanda said.

"Nothing. I ate some bad Thai food a few days ago and it's still wreaking havoc on my stomach," Lucy said. "Yesterday I threw up so much, I swear I puked up food I ate last week."

"Gross," Amanda said. She smoothed down her dress. "Maybe we shouldn't go tonight. I'd be fine with staying here and watching a movie."

"No way," Lucy said. "I've been looking forward to this all week. Besides, we told Gina we'd be there."

"It's only drinks at the bar," Amanda said. "And the rest of the salon will be there so it's not like we're leaving Gina alone."

Lucy studied her carefully. "Honey, I'm worried about you."

"I'm fine."

"You're not fine. I thought you were going to call Max yesterday and talk it out."

"I tried," Amanda said miserably. "He actually answered his phone and we talked for a bit, but he was so distant. It's been three days and he's still upset with me and I don't know how to fix this."

Lucy hugged her. "Which is why you need to go out with us tonight and get your mind off of Max. We're going to dance, eat greasy food, and you and Jason are going to drink copious amounts of liquor and then I'll drive your drunk asses home."

"I thought Jason was the designated driver tonight."

"He was," Lucy said as she studied her hair in the mirror, "but I'm not risking drinking tonight – not with the way my stomach feels. I've vomited enough the last few days, thank you."

"Max! Max, over here!" Gina stood up from the bar stool and waved excitedly.

78

Amanda stared at Lucy in panic as Max joined them in the crowded bar.

"I'm so glad you could make it!" Gina said before linking her arm around his.

"Thanks for inviting me," Max said. He smiled stiffly at Amanda before giving Lucy and Jason a more natural one. "Hey, you two."

"Hi, Max," Lucy said.

Jason grinned at him. "You're just in time for tequila shots."

Max laughed. "I haven't drunk tequila since university."

"What?" Gina said. "Well, it's time we changed that."

She slid a shot of tequila toward him and handed him a wedge of lemon. "Time to drink and suck, big guy."

Amanda watched as Max drank the shot before sucking on the lemon. Gina, her face squinched up, sucked at her lemon as well before grinning at Bethany. "Bethany, you didn't drink yours."

Bethany made a face. "I hate tequila, you know that."

"Oh, c'mon," Gina said. "We're partying tonight. Angie, order us another round, would you?"

The chubby brunette laughed and flagged down the waitress as Amanda stared at her shot of tequila.

"You gonna drink that?" Jason nudged her and she smiled at him before sliding it over to him.

"No, be my guest."

He grinned at her and downed the shot before nuzzling Lucy's neck affectionately. She put her arm around him and pressed a quick kiss against his mouth as Max said, "Excuse me for a minute. I'll be right back."

He disappeared toward the bathrooms and Amanda waited a few minutes before sliding from her bar stool and weaving her way around the people in the bar. She waited at the entrance to the bathroom hallway and when Max appeared, she touched his arm tentatively.

"Max?"

"Hey, Amanda," he said.

"Hi, how are you?"

"Good, you?"

She took a deep breath. "Awful. I hate that we're fighting."

"We're not fighting."

"We are," she said. "I'm so sorry for what I said. I truly didn't mean it the way it sounded but I – I know how it came across and I'm sorry."

"I'm sorry for being an asshole and ignoring you," he said.

"It's fine," she said. "I deserved it."

"You didn't."

"I did," she said. "You're a wonderful guy and if you want to date Gina, I think that's great."

He frowned at her. "I'm not interested in -"

"In fact," her stomach churning, she forced herself to go on, "tonight, I'm making it my mission to help you get to know Gina better. She's a really sweet girl and I think you two would make a cute couple."

"Amanda, you don't have to do that."

"I want to," she said. "We're friends, right?"

"Yes."

"Right, and what do friends do?"

"What?"

She forced a smile to her face. "They help their friends get laid. Come on, big guy, I'm gonna be your wingman tonight."

Before he could reply, she took him by the arm and led him back to their table. She planted him next to Gina and smiled at the receptionist before tugging on her blue locks. "Gina, did you know that Max plays paintball?"

"Really?" Gina squealed. "Max, I love paintball! In fact, I belong to a group that meets once a month at Paintball Plaza. You'll have to come with me and meet the gang. We're always looking for new members."

"That sounds nice," Max said with a quick look at Amanda.

She smiled and winked at him before nudging Gina. "You should tell Max about your Crossfit training, he mentioned he was looking for a new workout routine."

"Oh my God, you have to try Crossfit!" Gina said. She patted the bar stool beside her, and Max sat down as she pressed her slender body against his. "It's so amazing, Max."

As Gina chattered happily to him, Amanda moved back to her seat beside Lucy. The brunette frowned at her. "What are you doing?"

"Helping Max get laid," Amanda said.

"What?" Lucy gave her a look of disbelief as Jason snickered.

"What – what?" Amanda said.

"Why are you doing that?"

"Because we're friends and he and Gina like each other. Why wouldn't I?" Amanda said.

Lucy stared so long at her that she could feel her cheeks starting to heat up. She stared at the table and blocked out the sound of Gina's voice.

"Amanda," Lucy said in a low voice, "honey, I don't think -"

"It's *fine*, Luce," Amanda said. "We're friends again and I want to do something to make up for what I said to him."

"Setting him up with another woman when you want to fuck his brains out isn't a good idea," Lucy said.

"Ooh, snap," Jason said before laughing again.

"You're drunk already," Lucy said to him.

He nodded. "Yup, I am."

"I don't want to fuck his brains out," Amanda muttered. "Just let it go, Lucy. I'm being a good friend."

AMANDA CHECKED HER CELL PHONE BEFORE HANDING THE bartender a few bills and picking up her glass of club soda. It was close to eleven and, after watching Gina flirt with Max for the last three hours, she was more than ready to go home. She had been tempted to down alcohol until it no longer bothered her to see Gina and Max getting along so well, but she had resisted the urge. She wasn't entirely sure she wouldn't say something she'd regret if she was drunk. Instead, she had a couple glasses of wine before switching to club soda.

She slipped past a couple who were kissing passionately in the middle of the bar and headed for their table. Maybe she could convince Lucy it was time to go. Lucy was looking a little pale and she had disappeared to the bathroom a few times. Amanda had the feeling that she was vomiting again.

She set her drink on the table as Gina, giggling loudly, climbed into Max's lap. Hot and unpleasant jealousy flooded Amanda's belly when Gina pressed her mouth against Max's. Her coworkers hooted and catcalled and Amanda squeezed Lucy's arm as bile rose in her throat.

"Be right back," she mumbled. "I need some fresh air."

She turned and stumbled away with her vision weirdly shimmering. She made a beeline for the exit sign across the bar. She pushed at the door, nearly falling out into the cool night air when it opened. She slammed the door behind her before staggering away and leaning against the rough brick wall. She was in the alley behind the bar, and she stared up at the night sky, willing herself not to cry as anger and jealousy seethed through her.

The door opened and Max stepped out. She immediately turned and darted for the mouth of the alley. He caught her by the arm, pulling her to a stop as she tried to tug free.

"Let me go, Max."

"What's wrong?"

"Nothing," she said. "I needed some fresh air."

"I didn't kiss Gina," he said. "She kissed me."

"I don't care," she said. "You can kiss whoever the hell you want to kiss."

"You're jealous."

"No, I'm not," she denied hotly.

"You are. Why? You were the one who decided Gina and I made a cute couple, remember?"

"I'm not jealous," she insisted. "Did you like kissing her?" She winced at the spiteful tone in her voice.

"I have no interest in Gina," he said.

Her mouth dropped open, and she stared at him. "What the hell, Max?"

"I tried to tell you that when you decided to play wingman, but you wouldn't listen," he said. "Now I have to go back in there and convince Gina that I'm not taking her home tonight because she's too drunk to pick up on my body language."

She yanked her arm free. "I don't know what the hell you want from me, Max. First you're mad because I don't want you dating Gina and now you're mad because I do."

"If you had listened to me," he said patiently, "you would have -"

"What do you want from me?" Her anger and her jealousy were boiling over, and she scowled up at him. "You tell me what you want, and I'll do it."

She squeaked in surprise when he took her arm in a rough grip and pulled her away from the door. He backed her up against the brick wall and pinned her arms above her head before lowering his mouth to hers.

She could feel his warm breath on her lips, and she stared wide-eyed at him as he glared at her. "Do you really want to know, Butterfly?"

"Yes," she whispered. Little tingles of lust were zipping up and down her spine and she didn't object when Max shoved one large thigh between hers.

"I want to hear you admit that you want me as much as I want you," he said in a low voice. "I want to know that you spend most of your day thinking about what it would be like to have my dick deep inside your tight pussy. I want to know that when we're together, you picture us naked and fucking."

"Max," she moaned, "we're friends and -"

"Yes," he whispered before moving his mouth to her ear. He sucked on her earlobe and she made a low sound of need. "We're friends because I'm a nice guy, right?"

"Y-yes."

He let his mouth hover over hers and she parted her lips. He licked her bottom lip, and she pressed her pelvis against him as he licked her top lip.

"What if I stopped being a nice guy? What if I said to hell with being your friend and fucked you right here against the wall?"

"Oh God," she moaned.

"Do you think about fucking me?" he asked.

She hesitated before nodding.

"Say it," he said.

"I – I think about fucking you."

"Do you wonder how it would feel to have my cock in your pussy?"

"Yes," she breathed.

"Do you think your little pussy could take all of my dick?"

"I don't know," she whispered.

"But you want to find out. Don't you, Butterfly? You want to know if your pussy could take every inch of my cock. Don't you?"

"Yes. God, yes," she moaned.

Her eyes widened when his hand slipped under her dress. She tried to close her legs, glancing frantically around the empty alley, but his big thigh was still between hers and it kept her wide open to him. He stroked her inner thigh and sucked on her bottom lip.

"Are you wet for me, Butterfly?"

"Max, please," she whispered.

She gasped when he pushed his hand into her panties and cupped her naked pussy. He explored the small patch of blonde hair at the top of it before running his fingers over the smooth lips of her pussy. He probed between them, his rough fingers finding her clit, and covered her mouth with his when she made a harsh cry of pleasure. He kissed her, his tongue exploring every inch of her mouth as he caressed her clit into a swollen, throbbing bundle of nerves.

He pulled his hand free as he released her mouth and she gave him a trembling look of need as he studied her swollen lips. She watched wide-eyed as he brought his fingers to his mouth and sucked the moisture from one finger. Lust, so strong it made her pelvis hurt, rippled through her and he grinned at her before pushing his second finger into her mouth.

"Suck," he said.

She cleaned his finger, licking away her taste with her small pink tongue. He groaned and rubbed his erection against her.

"Do you want me to fuck you, Butterfly?" He released her arms before hooking his hands under her arms and lifting her until she was face-to-face with him. He held her up with one arm around her waist as she wrapped her legs around his hips.

"Well?" He nipped at her bottom lip before sucking and biting his way down her throat. She moaned, her hands clenching into his big shoulders. "Answer me, Butterfly. Do you want me to fuck you right here in the alley?"

"Yes," she suddenly hissed at him. "Fuck me right here, Max."

He pushed his hand up her dress again and into her panties. The sound of her cry echoed in the alley when he pushed two fingers deep inside her wet entrance.

"You're nice and tight, Butterfly," he said. "There's nothing I love more than a wet, tight pussy clinging to my dick."

"Fuck," she whispered as he pushed his fingers in and out of her. "Oh God."

She tensed when he pressed a third finger against her entrance. He nibbled on her neck. "If you can't take three of my fingers, you won't be able to take my cock."

"I can," she panted. "Just give me a minute."

He laughed, a low sound that sent shivers down her spine, before carefully easing his third finger into her pussy. She clenched around his fingers and he made a pleased noise. "Your pussy is so greedy, Butterfly."

"Your cock," she moaned. "Please, Max, I want it."

"Not yet," he said. "First you're going to fuck my fingers and show me how much you want my dick."

He pushed his fingers in and out and she met each of his strokes with a frantic thrust of her pelvis.

"Very good, Butterfly," he rumbled into her ear before biting her lobe.

She clung to him, burying her face into his thick neck to muffle her loud cries as he fucked her with his fingers and rubbed her clit with his thumb. Max, the nicest guy she knew, was finger fucking her in a filthy alley and she was about to come all over his hand. She arched her back, her breath coming in harsh, hot pants as he nipped at her neck.

"When you come, I want you to scream my name," he muttered into her ear. "I want everyone in the goddamn bar to hear you. Do you understand, Butterfly?"

She nodded, her pelvis thrusting back and forth against his fingers as he pressed on her clit with his thumb. She was so close. She took a deep breath and –

"Hey, Amanda? Are you ready to – shit."

She looked to her right, her eyes widening with horror when she saw Jason, weaving slightly, step out into the alley. He stared stunned at the two of them before abruptly whipping around. He weaved again, nearly falling over, and caught himself against the wall.

"So sorry," he said as Max pulled his hand free and lowered her to the ground. She straightened her dress as Max cursed under his breath.

"Sorry!" Jason said again. "I didn't realize you two were, uh…"

"Talking," Amanda said. "We were just talking."

Jason snorted laughter. "I'm not that drunk, Amanda."

"Fuck," she muttered. Jason had just seen her with Max's hand up her dress and she didn't know whether to laugh or cry.

"Lucy sent me out here to see if you were ready to leave.

She isn't feeling so great," Jason took a cautious look over his shoulder before turning around to face them, "and she's ready to go home."

He leaned against the wall and grinned at Max. "Don't eat at the House of Thai – ever. Anyway, you ready to go, Amanda? Or do you have," he paused and Amanda turned bright red when he winked at her, "other plans?"

"I'll give her a ride home," Max said.

"Perfect. I'll let Luce know." Jason reached for the door.

"Max, you don't have to -"

"I'll give you a ride home," he said. She shut her mouth with a snap as Jason opened the door to the bar.

"Have fun," he said before disappearing.

"Max -"

"Let's go, Amanda."

He took her hand and led her back into the bar. Lucy and Jason were already gone but Gina and the rest of the salon employees were still sitting at the table.

Gina smiled at Max. "Where'd you go, big guy? I was missing you."

She reached for his hand, frowning a little when he reached past her and grabbed Amanda's purse. He handed it to her and gave Gina a faint smile. "Amanda's not feeling well. I'm going to take her home."

"What?" Gina frowned. "Amanda, you're sick?"

"Um, yeah," Amanda said.

"Well, Lucy and Jason just left. You could probably catch a ride home with them and then Max can stay a little longer," Gina said.

Max shook his head. "No thanks, Gina. I need to get Amanda home. Good night, everyone."

Without waiting for their replies, he walked away. Amanda, her hand still stuck firmly in his, stumbled after him. He hurried her across the parking lot, and she squeezed his hand when he unlocked his truck.

"Max? How much have you had to drink? Maybe I should be driving."

"I had two shots and a beer two hours ago," he said. "I'm fine. Get in the truck, Amanda."

"Max, maybe this isn't a good idea."

He yanked open the passenger door and lifted her into the truck. He buckled her seat belt before climbing behind the wheel and driving out of the parking lot.

CHAPTER 6

"Th-thank you for the ride home," Amanda said.

Max unbuckled his seat belt, and she gave him a nervous look. "Thanks again, I'm sorry for earlier."

"Invite me in, Butterfly," he said in a low voice.

"That's probably not a good idea," she said. "What happened earlier -"

"Invite. Me. In."

"Max, won't you please come in?" she whispered.

The door to her townhouse was barely shut behind them before Max heaved her over his shoulder. He climbed the stairs and she tapped him on the back.

"What are you doing?"

"I told you, Butterfly, I'm done with being nice."

A funny little thrill went through her and her nipples hardened in anticipation as he set her on her feet in her bedroom. He bent over her and cupped her face in his hard hands, staring intently at her.

"I need to fuck you," he said.

"Max, our friendship -"

"I don't want to be your friend tonight. I want to be the guy who fucks you until you're screaming my name."

She made a soft whimper of need and he brushed his lips against hers. "Tell me you need me to fuck you, Butterfly."

She hesitated, lust and desire making her limbs tremble. He sighed angrily. "After tonight, we can go back to being friends."

She stared silently at him before whispering, "I need you to fuck me."

He kissed her immediately, touching his tongue against her crooked tooth before sliding his tongue past it and deep into her mouth. She returned his kiss, yanking at his shirt as he unzipped her dress. He dragged it down her body and quickly unclipped her bra, dropping it on the floor before cupping her breast in one big hand and kneading it.

She pulled again at his shirt and he stripped it off. She ran her hand over the hair on his chest as he unbuckled his belt and unbuttoned his pants. He shoved them down his legs, taking his briefs with him and she stared wide-eyed at his cock.

"Jesus, Max," she whispered.

He didn't reply, simply stepped out of his pants and grabbed his wallet from the back pocket. He pulled out a condom and set it on the bedside table before holding out his hand to her. "Come here, Butterfly."

She stared at his cock. He was very big and while she wasn't surprised by that, she was surprised by her reaction. She should have been nervous but instead she was consumed by a red-hot need to have his cock inside of her. She had no idea if she could take all of him but holy hell, she really wanted to find out.

She took his hand and he squeezed it reassuringly before tugging down her panties. She stepped out of them and he lifted her up and set her on her knees on the bed. They were almost face-to-face now and he cupped her breast before kissing her again. She pressed herself against him, his cock rubbing against her flat belly as he pulled on one nipple with his hard fingers.

She moaned and arched her back, digging her hands into his hair when he dipped his head and licked the tip of one aching nipple. He sucked it into his mouth, laving it with his tongue before nipping it with his teeth, and she made a harsh cry of need.

He pushed his hand between her legs, rubbing her pussy before whispering against her mouth, "I'm going to make you come first, Butterfly. I want you nice and wet when I fuck you."

She moaned again, spreading her thighs and leaning against him as he rubbed her clit with the pads of his fingers. She was already on the edge of climaxing and she gave him a desperate look of hunger when he slowed his fingers.

"Please," she pleaded, "I'm so close."

He grinned at her and kissed her as he rubbed her clit again. She screamed into his mouth, her entire body shaking as fire and lightning coursed through her veins. He held her up easily when she collapsed against him.

"Holy shit," she muttered. She sat back on the bed, watching as he rolled on the condom before lying on his back on the bed beside her.

"Straddle me, Butterfly," he said. "It's time to find out if your sweet little pussy can take my cock."

A little embarrassed by her eagerness, she scrambled onto his large body and grasped his cock. She stroked it, a thrill going through her when he immediately groaned and arched into her hand. She rubbed her thumb over the wide head before stroking him again and he caught her hand and pulled it away.

"I don't want a handjob," he said. "I want your pussy."

She nodded and he gripped her waist and lifted her. She braced one hand on his chest and held the base of his cock with her other, guiding it to her entrance as he lowered her onto him. They made mutual moans of pleasure as the head of his cock disappeared inside of her. Her knees touched the bed and she waited as she stretched around him.

"Okay?" he asked hoarsely.

"Yes," she said. "Just give me a minute."

She pushed down, taking more of his cock. She dug her fingers into his chest at the delicious feel of him filling her up. She had taken half of his dick and she glanced up at him, her body trembling at the look on his face.

"More," he rasped. "You can take more."

Moaning with pleasure, she pushed before lifting and pushing again. They both groaned and, her fingers digging into his chest, she pushed harder until his entire cock was sheathed inside of her.

She sat completely still. Her pussy was aching pleasantly, and she felt stretched and full to the brim. A stupid thrill of pride went through her when Max stroked her thighs and whispered, "I knew you could take all of it, Butterfly."

"Does it feel good?" she said.

"Yes," he said. "You're so tight and smooth. Your pretty pussy fits my cock perfectly."

She waited a moment longer before bracing her hands on his hard chest and riding him with slow, gentle thrusts. He held her hips loosely, letting her control the pace, and she smiled down at him before bouncing a little harder and faster.

He groaned, his hips rising to meet hers. She leaned over him and brushed her nipples against his chest. He groaned again before cupping both and caressing them. He tugged on her nipples, smiling when they hardened.

"I've dreamed about your breasts," he said. "How they would look in my hands, what colour your nipples are - how they would taste."

He urged her forward and she moaned when he sucked on first one nipple and then the other. He traced circles around them with his tongue and she gasped with pleasure before straightening and riding him hard.

He met her thrust for thrust, his hands digging into her hips and holding her tightly as she rode him with hard and furious strokes. She jerked, her pussy squeezing around him when his fingers touched her aching clit and he muttered a curse before rubbing her.

"I'm going to come if you keep doing that," she warned him breathlessly.

"Yes," he muttered. "Come all over my cock."

She shuddered again, her pace increasing as he rubbed and tugged at her clit and the familiar warmth started in her belly. She clung to his forearms, bouncing up and down as he pushed her closer and closer to the edge.

Her legs were beginning to tremble and as the pleasure washed over her in a huge roaring rush, she screamed his name and squeezed compulsively around him. He uttered another harsh curse and she was only vaguely aware of his hips pumping against her and his large body shaking beneath hers. She collapsed against him, resting her cheek against his chest and listening to the harsh thud of his heart as he thrust slowly twice more before relaxing on the bed. He rubbed her naked back and squeezed her ass before lifting her off of him. She was as limp as a noodle and he placed her on the bed before standing and disappearing into the bathroom.

He returned a few minutes later and she reached out and grabbed his hand. "Please don't leave, Max."

"I'm not going anywhere, Butterfly," he said before curling up behind her. He pulled the covers over them and spooned her, cupping one small breast in his large hand before kissing the back of her neck.

"Good night, Max."

"Good night, Amanda."

SHE WOKE TO THE TOUCH OF MAX'S HAND ON HER HIP. HE was still spooned behind her and she moaned when his erection pressed between her ass cheeks.

"Max," she said sleepily, "what time is it?"

"Late," he said. He pulled her against him and cupped her breast, tugging on her nipple until it was hard and swollen. He caressed both of her breasts as he kissed her neck and shoulder. She arched her back, panting harshly and pressing her ass against his cock.

He cupped her face and turned it toward him, kissing her before saying, "Are you ready to be fucked again, Butterfly?"

She reached out and slid open the nightstand drawer, snagging a condom from it and holding it up. He took it and she waited impatiently as he opened it. He moved down on the bed and caressed her smooth thigh before lifting it and draping it back over his hip. She groaned at the strain and he made a low chuckle and rubbed her aching thigh.

"I'm going to enroll you in yoga," he teased.

"There's no way in hell I'm doing – oh fuck!"

Her entire body arched as Max's warm hand cupped her pussy and rubbed at her clit.

"So wet already," he said, and she flushed brightly.

She *was* wet, embarrassingly so, but Max's body, his low voice and his naughty words were unbelievably sexy. She'd had sex with him only a few hours ago and already she was craving more. That had never happened with previous boyfriends.

He's not your boyfriend, remember?

She twitched as guilt flooded through her. She shouldn't be doing this to Max. He wanted a relationship, a commitment, and she couldn't give that to him.

"Max," she said hoarsely, "maybe we shouldn't -"

Her voice cut out and she forgot what she was going to say as the head of Max's cock slid into her wet pussy.

He lifted her leg higher, holding it up with his forearm and keeping her wide open to him as he thrust into her. There was a delicious feeling of fullness with a slight edge of pain, and she wiggled a little. Being on top meant she could control the pace and how much she took of him but in this position, he was in control. As he thrust again, she gave him a slightly panicked look.

"Max, it's too big. I can't take all of it in this position."

"Yes, you can." He kept a firm grip on her leg. "You're going to take all of my cock like a good girl, Amanda."

Her mouth dropped open, and she stared wide-eyed at him as a thread of dark and delicious pleasure shivered its way up her spine. The Max she knew was sweet and polite and never did anything she didn't want him to do. This Max, the one still slowly and carefully sliding his cock into her pussy despite her protests, was almost a stranger to her.

So why the fuck was she so turned on by it?

He dropped his hand to her pussy and she cried out with pleasure when he rubbed her clit.

"Do you want to come first? Is that it, greedy girl?" he asked.

He pinched her clit and a fresh surge of moisture helped him thrust a few more inches into her pussy. He rubbed her clit again, this time using the tips of his fingers and circling lightly. She clutched at his thick arm, her nails digging into his skin as he brought her closer.

"Max, oh, please," she begged when he stopped the gentle pressure.

"No," he said. "You only get to come once you've taken all of my cock."

She pouted at him and he slapped her lightly on the ass. "Take every inch, Butterfly, and then I'll let you come."

"Max, be nice," she said with another pout.

He grinned at her. "You don't like it when I'm nice, remember?"

"I like it," she panted as he stroked her clit with a maddeningly light touch.

He continued to push steadily into her and she squeezed his forearm as she stretched around him.

"Do you want my cock, Amanda?" He asked.

"Yes. I want it – all of it," she moaned.

"Then take it," he demanded.

This time when he thrust forward she pushed back to meet him and they both watched as her pussy slowly took his cock. When he was fully inside of her, his pelvis snug against her ass, he kissed the middle of her back.

"Well done, Butterfly."

That little tingle of stupid pride was back. She bit her bottom lip before moaning, "You're so thick, Max."

"I am," he agreed arrogantly. "And that's exactly what your little pussy needs, isn't it?"

"Yes," she said.

He kissed her back again before caressing her clit. She cried out with pleasure and he licked up her spine as his fingers stroked her. She thrust against him frantically, feeling the stretch of her muscles as his cock pushed in and out. When her climax rushed through her, she screamed and tightened compulsively around him.

He waited until the last of her climax shuddered through her before releasing her leg and grabbing her hip. "Keep your legs closed," he demanded.

She did as he asked, squeezing a handful of sheets as he fucked her roughly. His hot breath puffed across her naked back and the low moans he made as he fucked her were ratcheting up her desire to an almost unbearable level.

"Max," she muttered, "Oh God, Max."

He thrust repeatedly, a thick slide and retreat that made her pussy throb with need. She had always been hit and miss when it came to climaxing from sex alone, but as tiny beats of pleasure began in her lower body, she shoved her hips eagerly back and forth.

"Going to come again, Butterfly?" Max said.

She nodded, pushing back her hair impatiently when it stuck to her face. "Harder."

He laughed and held her hip before thrusting harder. Her body shook with the impact, but she moaned happily and held his arm as he fucked her. Her stomach tightened, her legs trembled, and she dug her nails deep into his flesh as the wave of pleasure washed over her. Behind her, Max made a harsh groan and shoved into her so deeply that she felt a brief pulse of pain. He groaned again, his entire body stiffening as he came before he collapsed against her. His weight knocked her onto her face and she made a muffled noise of protest. He hurriedly sat up and flipped her onto her back.

"Sorry, Butterfly."

"That's okay," she murmured.

She was feeling warm and weak and very sleepy, and a

soft smile crossed his face before he leaned down and kissed her. "Get some more sleep."

She nodded in agreement and when he relaxed on his back, she snuggled into him, resting her head on his chest and slinging her arm around his waist. He rubbed her back, and she made a soft noise of contentment before closing her eyes.

"Shit! I'm going to be late!" Amanda bounced out of the bed as Max sat up and blinked sleepily at her.

It was nine-thirty and her shift at the salon started at ten. She ran naked to the bathroom and quickly brushed her teeth before jumping into the shower. Ten minutes later she was back in the bedroom and dressing hurriedly. Max was still in her bed, in fact he was asleep again and snoring softly, and she leaned over him and rubbed his chest.

"Max? I have to go to work."

"Mmm," he muttered before rolling onto his side and pulling the covers over his head. She laughed and tugged them back before kissing him on the forehead. "Don't forget to lock the door when you leave."

He nodded and she hesitated for a moment. "Max, we're, uh, back to just friends today, right?"

He blinked before nodding. "Yeah."

"Thank you for last night. I – I really enjoyed it," she said.

There was a look she couldn't quite decipher on his face and her stomach began to churn with nausea. She should never have slept with Max last night, already it was getting awkward and –

He suddenly grinned at her – a grin she had grown to love - and held out his fist. "It was my pleasure, Amanda."

She stared at his fist before smiling and bumping it with hers. He collapsed back on the bed. "Have a good day at work."

"Thanks, Max. I'll talk to you later."

"You bet." He pulled the covers over his head again and she stood and walked out of the bedroom, forcing herself not to look back.

"HEY, HOW ARE YOU FEELING?" GINA ASKED WHEN SHE CAME flying into the salon at ten after ten.

"Better," Amanda said. She checked the appointment book as she tucked her purse under the desk. Thankfully her first appointment wasn't until ten-thirty. She hurried to the coffee machine and poured herself a cup of coffee. Her thighs were aching and she rubbed them as Gina joined her.

"So, I had a great time with Max last night," Gina said. "I'm thinking of asking him out."

Jealousy clawed through her stomach and she forced a smile to her face. "Oh yeah?"

Gina nodded. "He's so sweet and good looking. Honestly, I don't know why you're not dating him."

"He's my friend," Amanda said.

"I know," Gina said. "Maybe you and I could have coffee after work tonight and you can give me some hints on what Max is like. You know him better than anyone."

"I have plans after work. Sorry," Amanda said.

"Maybe tomorrow?" Gina said. "It's Sunday and I don't have any plans in the afternoon. Maybe we could -"

"I'm busy all weekend," Amanda said.

"Oh, okay. Well, I guess I'll have to use old-fashioned charm to win him over," Gina said.

The phone rang and Amanda breathed a sigh of relief when Gina ran to answer it. It didn't bother her that Gina wanted to date Max but she sure as hell wasn't going to help her do it.

Bullshit. It bothers you. The only reason you're not trying to beat the crap out of her is because Max told you he wasn't interested in Gina.

She sighed inwardly. Now that she was away from Max and his hard body and filthy mouth, she was already starting to feel guilty about what she had done. Why had she slept with him? Even if they could forget about what had happened and just be friends again, the thought of Max in bed with another woman made her ridiculously jealous. She didn't want him talking dirty to anyone but her, dammit.

She pulled her cell phone from her pocket and quickly texted Lucy. She needed to talk to her best friend, and she prayed like hell that Lucy could meet her for lunch.

"SAY SOMETHING, LUCY," AMANDA SAID.

Lucy stared at her uneaten salad for a moment before studying Amanda. "You slept with Max."

"Yes."

"Twice."

"Yes."

"And now you're back to just being friends."

"Yes."

Lucy continued to stare at her, and Amanda groaned. "I know, I fucked up."

"No, you fucked Max," Lucy said before grinning at her. "Although, honestly, I'm not surprised. Jason told me about catching you two in the alley and that Max had you pinned against the wall with his hand up your dress."

"Oh my God," Amanda groaned. "I'll never be able to look Jason in the eye again."

"It's not that big of a deal," Lucy said. "How was it?"

"What?"

"How was it? Did you enjoy it? Was his dick as giant-sized as the rest of him?"

"Lucy! Keep your voice down." Amanda looked around the busy café.

Lucy laughed and leaned forward. "Well, answer me."

"It was unbelievably good. I enjoyed it way more than I should have, and yes, he's, uh, large."

"How large?"

"Very large," Amanda said. "Now focus – did I make a really bad mistake?"

"Do you think you did?"

"I don't know," Amanda said. "Part of me says yes, absolutely, but the other part of me wants to…"

"Keep fucking his giant dick?" Lucy said.

Amanda glared at her and Lucy snickered. "Sorry, honey. Listen, for what it's worth – I'm not surprised that you two finally slept together and my personal opinion is that you should keep sleeping together."

"Max was very clear last night and this morning that we would go back to being friends."

"Maybe he said what he thought you wanted to hear." Lucy pushed her salad around her plate with her fork. "He's obviously attracted to you. Give it a chance, honey. I know you have this thing about him being nice but -"

"He's not nearly as nice when he's in my bed."

"Oh?" Lucy raised her eyebrows. "Go on."

"He says dirty things. Not to get too personal but when

we were, um, in a certain position and I said I couldn't, uh, take all of him he ignored me and basically said I was going to be a good girl and take every inch."

"Max said that?" Lucy gave her a look of disbelief.

"Yes," Amanda said. "He's like a completely different person in bed, Luce. He's a little bit rough and demanding, and fuck if I don't love every damn minute of it."

"As long as you like it, I don't see what the problem is."

"I like it too much, that's the problem."

"Say, is it awkward with the height difference? How did you two even have sex?" Lucy asked.

Amanda grinned at her. "It's like Doris says – you have to be creative."

"Who the hell is Doris?"

"It's a long story," Amanda said. She stared at Lucy's plate. "You haven't eaten a thing. Are you still feeling sick?"

Lucy nodded. "Yeah."

"It must be the flu. Food poisoning doesn't go on this long. Maybe you should go to the doctor."

"I have an appointment on Monday," Lucy said.

"Good." Amanda reached out and touched Lucy's hand. "Tell me what's wrong, Lucy."

Lucy stared at her plate. "I missed my period."

"What?"

"Actually, I've missed the last three periods."

"Holy shit," Amanda breathed. "Are you pregnant?"

Lucy shook her head. "No, I can't be."

"Did you take a test?"

"No. There's no point, Amanda. I have less than a five percent chance of getting pregnant. Most likely the infection has come back."

"Did you tell Jason?"

"No, I don't want him worrying until after I see the doctor. I'm sure I'll just have to go on antibiotics again."

"Lucy, you've been throwing up, remember?"

"Bad Thai food, remember?"

"Are you sure that's all it is?" Amanda asked. "You're throwing up, you've missed your period for the last three months, maybe you really are -"

"No," Lucy snapped. "I'm not pregnant, Amanda."

"I'm sorry," Amanda said.

"No, I'm sorry," Lucy said. "I didn't mean to snap at you. I just – I wish I was pregnant, you know? I hate that I…"

She dabbed at her eyes with her napkin. "Anyway, I'll go to the doctor on Monday and find out what's going on with my stupid body and then I'll talk to Jason."

She wiped again at her eyes before smiling at Amanda. "So, do you have plans with Max tonight?"

"Well, he normally comes over for dinner and we watch a movie but I'm not sure if that's going to happen. It was a bit awkward this morning when I left. God, I hope I haven't completely fucked up our friendship. If I – if I hurt Max, I'll never forgive myself."

Lucy squeezed her hand. "Maybe you shouldn't see him until you've figured out what it is you want from him."

Amanda nodded, even as her stomach dropped at the thought of not seeing him, "Yeah, you're right. I was going to text him about tonight, but I'll give him some space. He said he was okay with going back to friends but there was this look on his face for a minute that… I won't fuck this up, Lucy. I can't – Max is too important to me."

"I know, honey," Lucy said. "I know."

CHAPTER 7

She had just kicked off her shoes and was heading upstairs when there was a knock on the front door. It opened and Max, carrying two bags of groceries, stepped into the front hallway.

"Max? Wh-what are you doing here?"

He frowned at her. "It's Saturday night. Dinner and movie, remember?"

"Yes," she said. "I wasn't sure if you wanted to hang out with me tonight."

"Of course, I do."

She followed him into the kitchen, and he placed the bags on the counter. "Unless you don't want me here?"

"I do," she said. "What, uh, what's on the menu?"

"Grilled chicken in a lemon-dill sauce with roasted asparagus tips," he said.

"Sounds delicious."

"It's an old family recipe," he said with a grin. "I'm going to light the barbeque."

"Right. I'll go and change," she replied.

She walked upstairs, her heart thudding with excitement

and her cheeks flushed. Even though she had told herself on the drive home that she wouldn't text or call him, she was stupidly excited to see him. She stripped off her work clothes and was reaching for her yoga pants when she caught sight of herself in the full-length mirror. She hurried to her closet and hunted through it before pulling out the short sundress. She held it up to her body before tossing it on the bed and hurrying into the bathroom and taking off her bra and underwear.

What are you doing, Amanda?

Nothing. I just feel like dressing up a little tonight, that's all.

You're playing a dangerous game.

She ignored her inner voice and stepped into the shower.

MAX TOOK THE CHICKEN OFF THE BARBEQUE AND BROUGHT IT into the house. He stirred the sauce, tasting it quickly before shutting off the burner and pulling the asparagus from the oven. Amanda still hadn't returned from upstairs. He set the table, his stomach tight with nerves. After leaving her house this morning, he had convinced himself he wouldn't return tonight. He went to the gym and worked out, then cleaned his apartment and watched some TV. An hour before Amanda finished her shift at the salon, he showered and drove to the grocery store. He picked up the groceries, telling himself repeatedly that he would drive home and eat alone, but he had driven to Amanda's. She was walking into her townhouse and he'd sat for a moment in his truck.

What are you doing, Max?

Having dinner and a movie with my friend. Just like I do every Saturday.

She's more than a friend to you and do you really think you can go back to not touching her, not kissing her, after last night?

He'd ignored his inner voice and walked quickly to her house. She'd seemed surprised to see him but not upset and it calmed his nerves a bit. But now they were jangled again. Anxious and jittery, he decided to cut a bit more from the asparagus stalks. He grabbed the cutting board and the knife, using the tongs to line up the hot stalks neatly on the cutting board before beginning to slice through them.

"That smells good."

He turned, the smile dying on his lips, as he stared at Amanda. She was standing in the doorway of the kitchen, her long blonde hair piled on top of her head and the sweet scent of her strawberry body wash drifting to him. Instead of her usual yoga pants and t-shirt, she was wearing a short little sundress with thin straps. He stared at the curve of her neck, her bare shoulders, and the delicate line of her collarbone. His eyes drifted to her small breasts and his cock hardened in his jeans. Jesus, she wasn't wearing a bra. He swallowed with difficulty as he stared at the outline of her nipples against the fabric of her dress. He shouldn't have come here tonight. She was hard enough to resist in her yoga pants and t-shirt, he didn't stand a chance of resisting her in that skimpy little dress.

There was a sharp pain in his finger, and he glanced down. There was a drop of blood on the cutting board, small and unobtrusive and he stared curiously at it for a moment. Where did that come from? He caught sight of the blood welling from his index finger and took a staggering step back as the room spun. Dimly he could hear Amanda calling his name, but the world spun again and then went black.

When Amanda walked into the kitchen and Max's gaze dropped to her breasts, it sent lust skyrocketing through her. She wasn't wearing a bra and she knew perfectly well that it was noticeable. Hell, her nipples were rock hard and she could barely stop from moaning when Max stared hungrily at her chest. She was doing this to him on purpose, she wanted him to want her despite their agreement to go back to being friends. Guilt went through her when he turned away and stared at the cutting board on the counter.

Her eyes widened when Max took a staggering step back. "Max? Honey, what's wrong?"

He staggered again before turning slowly to face her. His eyes rolled back in his head and she shouted in alarm as he crumpled to the floor. Without thinking, she ran forward and caught him as he fell. His weight drove her to the floor with a hard thud and she cursed, her eyes watering with pain when the back of her head smacked the tile.

Max was lying half on top of her, his head cushioned on her abdomen and she touched his head. "Max, honey? Are you with me?"

There was no response and she dragged herself out from under him, supporting his head with one hand before easing it to the floor. She heaved him onto his back, her muscles straining from the effort, before rubbing at the back of her head and looking him over for injuries. He had cut his finger with the knife, but it wasn't deep and already starting to clot. She grabbed the first-aid kit from under the sink and cleaned the cut with some antiseptic spray before wrapping a Band-Aid around his finger. When the cut was covered, she wet a washcloth with cool water and sat on the floor beside him.

She wiped at his forehead and cheeks with the cool cloth before tapping him on the cheek.

"Max? Wake up, honey."

She could see his eyes rolling back and forth beneath his eyelids and she wiped his face again with the cloth before shaking his shoulder. "Open your eyes, Max."

His eyelids fluttered open, and he stared hazily at her. "Amanda?"

"Hi, honey."

"What happened?"

"You cut your finger and fainted." She wiped his forehead again with the cloth. "Do you think you can sit up?"

He nodded and she helped him into a sitting position, leaning him back against the cupboards before rubbing his chest. "How do you feel? Anything hurt?"

"Just my pride," he muttered.

"It's no big deal," she said.

He touched the scar on his face. "At least I didn't smash my face into the kitchen table."

She smiled and rubbed his chest again as he frowned at her. "I can't believe I didn't break my nose or something."

"I caught you."

He blinked at her. "You what?"

"I caught you when you fell." She grinned at him. "Well, mostly. I wasn't able to stay on my feet, but I at least broke your fall, so you didn't smash face-first into the tile floor."

"Amanda," he grabbed her arms and squeezed them, "don't ever do that again. I could have hurt you badly."

"It's no big deal, Max."

"It is," he insisted. "I could have broken your ribs when I landed on you. You should have let me fall."

"Like I was going to let you break your face on the floor.

I'm fine. You didn't hurt me." She decided not to tell him about smacking her head.

"But I could have," he said. "I could have hurt you and I -"

"You didn't," she said. "Stop worrying about it."

He cursed under his breath before glancing at the Band-Aid on his finger. "How bad is it?"

"Minor," she said. "But I thought it would be best to put some antibiotic spray and the Band-Aid on it before I woke you up."

His cheeks flushed a dull red. "I'm sorry, Amanda."

"You have nothing to be sorry about. You can't help if you faint at the sight of your own blood. Now, do you think you can stand up? You can have a seat at the table, and I'll dish up supper."

"I can do it," he said as he climbed to his feet.

"Nope. You sit down and drink some water. You can direct me as to how you want it to look," she said. "Sit down, Max."

He sat and she poured him a glass of water. He caught her hand as she moved away and said, "My manliness factor just hit an all-time low, didn't it?"

She shook her head and couldn't resist glancing at his crotch. "No, definitely not."

He cleared his throat. It was her turn to flush when she realized she was still staring at his dick, and she turned away quickly. "Let's eat. I'm starving."

"What's wrong?"

"Nothing," Amanda said. She shifted again on the couch before staring at the television. They had been watching *The*

Princess Bride for over an hour now and she couldn't seem to stop squirming. It was being so close to Max. His large thigh brushing against her bare one and the scent of his aftershave was driving her to distraction. She wanted him again, fuck did she want him. She could barely stop herself from climbing into his lap and kissing him.

She squirmed again, the fabric of the couch felt too rough against her sensitive skin and Max glanced at her. "You keep squirming."

"I can't get comfortable," she said.

His gaze dropped to her breasts and her nipples immediately hardened. She sucked in her breath, her fingers digging into her knees, as she watched a muscle tick in his temple. After a moment he looked away and she released her breath in a harsh sigh of disappointment.

She leaned casually against him, tucking her feet under her and smoothing her short dress over her thighs. He glanced at her bare legs, that ticking muscle back in his temple, before abruptly draining his bottle of beer and setting it on the coffee table.

He settled back into the couch and she leaned a little harder against him. He didn't put his arm around her, and she tried to ignore her trickle of disappointment. In the past he had occasionally put his arm around her, a friendly gesture more than anything. She desperately wanted him to do it again. When he didn't, she squirmed again, resisting the urge to straddle his thigh and rub her pussy against the lean, hard muscle.

That thought brought a surge of wetness to her panties and she cursed inwardly before sliding her legs out from under her and swinging them idly. She had to stop thinking about Max's body, about his thick cock, about the way he –

She jerked with surprise when Max abruptly hauled her

into his lap. He pressed her back against his chest and goose-bumps rose on her flesh when she felt his hot breath on her bare shoulder.

"Is that better?" he asked.

"Yes," Amanda said.

"Good, now watch the movie."

She leaned against his chest and stared at his big hands. They were resting casually on his thighs on either side of hers. She spread her thighs a little, so that they were touching his hands.

The movie, Amanda, concentrate on the movie.

Right, the movie. She forced her gaze to the screen, her legs jittery and restless. When Max rested his hands on the top of her thighs and casually stroked them, she lost what little interest she had in the movie.

"Max, wh-what are you doing?"

"You're still squirming," he said.

"Sorry."

He didn't reply, just kept rubbing the tops of her thighs with his warm hands.

Don't open your legs, Amanda, don't open your legs.

She definitely shouldn't spread her legs. She and Max were just friends. So, why were her thighs drifting further apart and why was she on pins and needles waiting to see if Max would notice her silent plea.

His hands continued to rub the tops of her thighs. She imagined she could almost hear the rasp of his skin against hers. She was starting to sweat a little and when his hands slipped to the inside of her thighs and rubbed, a soft little moan escaped her throat.

"You okay, Amanda?"

"Um, yes, why?"

"Just checking," he said. She could hear the amusement in

his voice and a flush of shame went through her. It wasn't enough to stop her pelvis from hitching forward each time his hands brushed her inner thighs.

Moving slowly, she spread her legs until they were dangling over his. She was wide open to him, her invitation perfectly clear, but still he continued to rub only the inside of her thighs. When he moved back to the tops of her legs, she made a grunt of frustration.

"Something wrong?" he asked.

"No, I -"

He shifted her on his lap and there it was, that hardness she was absolutely aching for pressing into her ass. She moaned and ground against it as Max's hands tightened on her thighs. She squirmed again and he slapped one thigh lightly.

"Be good, Butterfly."

"I am being good," she said.

"You're squirming."

"I'm warm," she said.

"Let me help you with that," he replied.

Dismay went through her. He was going to move her off his lap and that was the last thing she wanted. She twitched in surprise when instead of lifting her from his lap, he grabbed the bottom of her dress and yanked it over her head. Her arms dropped to cover her naked breasts instinctively and Max made a low sound of disapproval before tugging her arms away. He forced her back against his chest before resting his hands on her thighs again.

"This is my favourite part of the movie," he said as if she wasn't reclining on his lap in nothing but a skimpy thong.

"M-mine too," she stuttered. Her nipples were hard as rocks and she couldn't seem to stop panting.

"Still warm?"

"Um, no, it's better," she said.

"Good." He rubbed her thighs in a friendly way, and she arched her pelvis toward him. He didn't touch her pussy, but he did move his hands to her inner thighs again and trace the skin with his fingertips.

"Oh," she whispered when his fingers skimmed along the crease between her thigh and her pussy. "Please, Max."

"Your nipples are very distracting," he whispered into her ear. "They're just begging for my touch."

"Please," she said again.

He laughed and ran his hands up her ribcage before cupping both breasts and pulling at her nipples. "Is this better?"

"Yes!" she cried out as her back arched. She stared sight-lessly at the TV as Max rubbed and plucked her nipples.

Her panties were soaked through and she blushed when Max dropped his right hand and touched the growing damp spot on the silk.

"What's this?" he said teasingly. "You've ruined your panties."

"It's your fault," she said.

"My fault?" He traced the wet silk with his index finger. "How is it my fault?"

"Your cock," she moaned.

He laughed again. "Are you telling me that all you have to do is think about my cock and you ruin your panties?"

"Yes," she moaned again.

He cupped her face and turned it toward his, kissing her as he slid his hand inside her panties and cupped her wet pussy. He rubbed at her swollen clit before pulling his mouth from hers and wrapping his arm around her waist. She didn't object when he lifted her and pulled her thong down, and even helped him when it got stuck on her thighs. She pushed it down impatiently, kicking it off her feet, and Max kissed the back of her shoulder.

"Scoot forward, Butterfly."

She balanced on his knees, moaning when she heard the rasp of his zipper. His shirt landed on the floor beside the couch and he lifted his hips and pushed his jeans and briefs to his upper thighs, then pulled her back. She leaned against his naked chest, rubbing her ass against his cock as she shoved his clothes to his knees. He held her around the waist and stopped her from moving.

"Max! Fuck me!" she snapped.

"We're watching a movie, not fucking, Amanda."

"I don't care about the damn movie!"

"What?" He stared at her in mock horror. "It's one of your favourites."

"I don't care," she repeated through gritted teeth.

"We always watch a movie on Saturday night, remember?" He traced circles on her thighs.

"It's good to break a routine," she said.

He laughed, the sound reverberating against her naked back, before cupping her pussy. "Tell you what, Butterfly, I'm pretty good at multi-tasking so why don't I give your pussy my cock while we watch the movie?"

"Yes," she said. "That's a really great idea."

"Are you sure?" he teased. "I know you love this movie, and I don't want to distract you from it."

"I'm positive. One hundred percent positive," she said before reaching behind her and wrapping her hand around his thick cock. She stroked him, loving the sound of his low moan, and turned her head to kiss his throat. "Please, Max."

"Such sweet begging, Butterfly. How can I resist?"

He lifted her again – fuck, it was incredibly sexy the way

he could lift her and move her – and used his other hand to guide his cock to her pussy.

"Wait, we need a condom," she moaned as the blunt head touched her narrow entrance.

"I won't come," he said and lowered her onto his cock.

Like before, she could only take part of him before her hands were digging into his forearms. She made a harsh mutter of frustration as Max held her and she hovered on half his dick.

"Am I hurting you?"

"No, I just – I want to take all of you right away," she said.

He nuzzled the back of her neck before lowering her down a little further. "It's fine, Butterfly. It's better this way."

She braced her hands on his thighs, helping to support her body weight as he eased her up and down until her ass touched his lap and her pussy was full and stretched around his entire length.

"Ohh," she sighed. "God, that's good."

He rubbed her naked back before tugging her legs open until they dangled on either side of his. She rubbed his thighs encouragingly, but he didn't move. She was too short for her feet to touch the floor, so she had no leverage. Unless Max moved, she could do nothing but sit there stuffed full of his damn cock.

"Max," she said.

"Shh, Butterfly. I'm watching the movie."

"You said you'd fuck me while we watched the movie." She craned her neck to scowl at him over her shoulder.

"No," he said with a wicked grin, "I said I'd give your sweet little pussy my cock while we watched the movie. I did that."

"Asshole!" she snapped, and he laughed so hard his entire body shook.

She moaned when it made his cock rub against her inner walls. He put his arms around her and cupped her breasts. He teased her nipples as she closed her eyes and arched her back encouragingly.

"I feel like you're not even watching the movie, Amanda," he said.

"I am." Her eyes popped open, and she stared at the television as he toyed with her nipples. She squeezed her muscles around his cock, smiling when he moaned. She yelped when he pinched her nipple.

"Behave, Amanda."

"I am," she said before squeezing him again. He was so thick she wasn't entirely certain it made that much of a difference, but he inhaled and made a tiny thrust of his pelvis.

"Oh!" She stared over her shoulder at Max. "I liked that. Will you do it again?"

He leaned forward, his hard chest brushing against her naked back and kissed her as he kneaded her breasts.

"Watch the movie," he whispered against her mouth before releasing her breasts and leaning back against the couch. He grinned when she smacked him on the thigh in protest.

She faced forward again. It was time to take matters into her own hands. She had been working out at the gym for a few weeks now, she had some core strength for God's sake. She braced her hands on his thighs and raised herself up and down. It wasn't much movement – definitely not the hard strokes she longed for - but it was enough to send pleasure straight from her pussy to her toes.

Max's hands curled around her waist and she tensed, ready to punch him if he stopped her from moving. To her delight, he helped her. He held her firmly, providing support and extra lifting power so that she could bounce enthusiastically. She leaned forward further, her fingers digging into his legs, and rocked her pelvis back and forth. It felt a little precarious – she was leaning well over his legs and if he let her go, she'd fall off his lap and straight to the floor – but she knew Max wouldn't let her fall and the position was making his cock rub against the front wall of her pussy. It sent little shockwaves of pleasure up and down her legs and she tried to move faster. Her arms were starting to shake from exertion, and she muttered a curse.

Max moved one hand to the back of her neck and held tightly as he lowered his other hand from her waist to her hip. She was locked in his strong grip and she moaned her gratitude when he thrust back and forth. She rode him helplessly, each deep stroke of his cock sending fire licking along her veins and was only dimly aware that she was begging and pleading for him to fuck her harder.

She dragged oxygen into her lungs in harsh, rough pants and she heard Max curse under his breath when her unexpected and incredibly strong orgasm swept through her. She cried out, her entire body first stiffening and then shuddering around him as the pleasure radiated throughout her body. It seemed to go on forever and she twitched and squeezed around his cock uncontrollably until finally collapsing against his chest in a sweaty, moaning mess. He brushed away the strands of hair that were sticking to her face before kissing her cheek.

"That seemed like a good one."

"That was the best fucking orgasm of my life," she said.

"Good."

He was still thick and hard inside of her, but he made no

effort to move, just rubbed her arms before saying, "The movie is over."

She stared at the credits as he reached for the remote and shut off the television. "Do you want me to leave?"

She frowned at him. "Of course not."

A brief look of relief crossed his face and he kissed her before lifting her off his lap. He stood and pulled up his jeans and briefs. Still naked, she leaned against him and wrapped her arms around his waist. "Come to bed, Max."

They walked up the stairs to the bedroom and she smiled at him. "Round two?"

He laughed and nodded. "Hell, yes."

He studied her bed before studying her and she gave him a slightly self-conscious look. "What?"

He pulled her into his embrace and cupped her breast. "I'd really like to put you on your hands and knees and fuck you, but your bed is too low."

Desire, hot and heavy, pulsed through her and she said, "We could try propping some pillows under me."

"I don't think it'll be enough." He teased her nipple with the ball of his thumb. "If we were in my bedroom, you'd be on your hands and knees on my bed right now with my cock buried in your pussy."

She shuddered with pleasure and they kissed for long moments, their tongues tasting and teasing as she clung to him.

"I really think we should try," she said when he released her mouth.

He grinned teasingly. "I have a better idea. Why don't we make it lady's choice? You can fuck me however you want, Butterfly."

She bit her bottom lip, her hands tightening on his arms. "I like that idea. Lie on your back on the bed, Max."

He did what she asked, removing his clothes before stretching out, as she moved to the side of the bed. She reached under the mattress and he raised his eyebrows when she placed the restraint cuff that was tucked under the top mattress on the quilt. She moved to the other side of the bed and brought out the second cuff.

He was still staring at her and she blushed. "It's an under-the-bed restraint kit."

"I know what it is," he said.

"Do you trust me, Max?"

He held out his right arm to her in reply and she placed the fabric cuff around his wrist, securing it with the Velcro strips.

"Too tight?"

He shook his head no and she moved to the other side of the bed and secured his left wrist. He tugged experimentally at the bonds and she smiled at him. "Comfortable?"

"Very," he said.

"Good. Give me a safe word."

He thought for a moment. "Peanut butter."

"Peanut butter?"

He nodded and she laughed and patted his chest. "Peanut butter it is."

His cock was standing straight up, and she stared appreciatively at it before climbing onto the bed and straddling his waist. She rubbed her pussy against his abs before leaning over and offering her breast to him. He sucked on her nipple and when it was hard and throbbing pleasantly, she guided her other nipple to his mouth. He sucked obediently on it as she threaded her fingers through his thick hair and held him. She moaned, rocking her pussy against his hard abdomen as he sucked and licked.

She straightened and he stared hungrily at her. "Fuck me, Butterfly."

Her face broke out in a grin and she traced her fingers across the hair on his chest. "Not yet, handsome."

She leaned down and pressed warm, wet kisses against his chest. He groaned and when she licked one flat nipple, his pelvis bucked, and she had to squeeze him with her thighs to avoid falling.

"Do you like that?" she said.

He stared pleadingly at her and she sucked experimentally on his nipple. He cursed and bucked again, the muscles in his arms bulging as he pulled at the straps that held him captive.

"You do like that," she said.

"Butterfly," he warned, "you need to fuck me right now."

"And if I don't?" she said. "What are you going to do about it? You're tied to my bed and I can do whatever I want to you."

Her pussy dripped moisture onto his stomach and she wasn't the least bit embarrassed by it. Having Max tied to her bed was her number one fantasy and she was so turned on she could barely think straight.

Ignoring his muttered pleas, she kissed her way down his body, tasting and licking his warm, hard skin as he squirmed and jerked beneath her. He arched his back, and she licked each line of his ribs before straddling his thighs. She stared at his cock and he moaned when she leaned down and her small breasts brushed against it.

She pressed a line of kisses along his V-line, smiling at the way it made him cry out as his cock leaked precum all over her breasts. She straightened again and ran her thumb through the moisture on the head of his cock. She licked her thumb as a look of dark lust crossed his face before grasping the base of him in her hand. She stroked him, twisting the palm of her hand against the shaft as his pelvis rose and fell.

"Do you want my mouth, Max?" she said.

"Yes," he rasped. "God, yes."

"Not yet," she said.

He cursed and yanked again at his restraints. They held him tight, and she giggled. "I like having you tied to my bed."

"If you untie me, Butterfly, I'll eat your pussy."

"For how long?" she said.

"As long as you want me to," he said. "Untie me."

"The thing is," she said. "I don't have to untie you. Do I? You don't need your hands to eat my pussy."

"Amanda," he said as she knee-walked her way up the bed, "please untie me."

"Nope," she said. There wasn't a whole lot of space between Max's shoulders and the headboard but, moving carefully, she wedged her knees on either side of his head and smiled down at him. Her lower legs and feet were resting against his chest and she rubbed him with her left foot.

"Too heavy?" she asked.

"No," he said hoarsely. His hands were clenching and unclenching, and he was staring hungrily at her pussy. She reached between her legs and swiped two fingers across her wet lips before placing them at his mouth.

"Open."

He opened his mouth, and she slid her fingers into the warm recess, moaning when he sucked on them. She pulled her fingers free and lowered herself down until her pussy was just above his mouth. "Are you going to be a good boy and eat my pussy, Max?"

"Yes," he said.

She held onto the headboard with one hand and weaved the fingers of her other into his thick hair. She held his head as she lowered her pussy to his mouth. His warm, wet tongue slipped across her pussy lips and she moaned. He probed between her lips, the tip of his tongue finding her swollen clit and licking it delicately.

She moaned again and he flattened his tongue and licked her clit with slow, broad sweeps. She rocked back and forth, her hand pulling his hair and her toes digging into his chest. His beard scratched lightly at her inner thighs and pussy lips and the rough texture of it combined with the softness of his tongue heightened her pleasure. He worked her clit with slow and gentle licks, and she pulled his hair and muttered, "More."

He sucked on her clit, teasing it with the tip of his tongue as he sucked, and she made a harsh shriek of pleasure before grinding her pussy against his face. His tongue worked furiously against her clit as he sucked, and she made another shriek before riding his face to a hard and immensely satisfying orgasm.

Her legs trembling, she eased back. She steadied herself with one hand on his broad shoulder until she was straddling his waist. She used the sheet to wipe the moisture from his face and beard as he gave her an almost painful look of hunger.

"Such a good boy," she said before leaning over and kissing him. She could taste herself in his mouth and she rubbed her hard nipples against his chest as he kissed her frantically. When she straightened, he gave her another pleading look.

"Fuck me, Amanda."

"Soon," she said.

He cursed and glared at her. She rubbed her nose against his before sucking on his bottom lip. "Tormenting you is so much fun, Max."

He pulled again at the restraints and she nipped his thick neck. "Be still, honey."

He took a deep breath and his hands relaxed against the restraints.

"Good," she whispered.

She kissed her way down his body again until her mouth was hovering over his cock. He groaned at the feel of her warm breath and she smiled at him before taking the head of his cock into her mouth. His hips bucked up and she pulled away, giving him a disapproving look.

"Be still."

"I can't."

"You can."

She held the base of his cock and sucked on the head again, flicking her tongue against the slit as he moaned and cursed and pleaded. She took more, her lips stretching around his width and bobbed her head in a slow rhythm. His hips were rising and falling with her mouth and she reached between his legs and cupped his balls, stroking them as she licked his cock before sucking again. She moved faster, sucking hard, and he cried out as his ass rose off the bed. He yanked at the restraints and she smiled up at him when they held fast.

"Please, Butterfly, please," he begged. "Please fuck me."

"Such sweet begging, honey. How can I resist?" she said with a wicked grin.

She grabbed a condom from the nightstand and carefully slid it onto his cock, taking her time and pumping him with her hand when she was done.

He groaned. "I'm going to come all over your fucking hand if you don't stop."

"That's no fun," she chided. "Control, Max. You need to have control."

She stroked him a few more times, enjoying the way he gritted his teeth and stared grimly at the ceiling as he fought to keep from coming.

When he felt her warm pussy slide down over the head of his cock, he made a choked cry of need and she rubbed his abdomen. She was soaking wet, having Max under her control made her hotter than hell. To her surprise and delight, she slid smoothly down his entire cock in one push.

She waited a few seconds before rocking back and forth. The motion put delicious friction against her clit, and she gasped with pleasure before smiling at him. "I'm going to use your dick to make myself come. Don't you dare come with me."

"Amanda," he said in a strangled voice. "I don't think I can stop it."

"You can," she said. "I know you can."

"Fuck!" he snarled and she patted him on the abdomen before rocking back and forth.

"It won't take long," she panted. "I promise."

He groaned in response and when she cupped one small breast and tugged on her nipple, he immediately stared at the ceiling again, his entire body twitching under hers. She laughed before rocking again. In less than two minutes, she was coming wildly, her nails digging into Max's stomach and her entire body shuddering around him. He cried out when her pussy squeezed him and made a few helpless thrusts before he regained control.

When she had caught her breath and her limbs were no longer trembling quite so wildly, she smiled at him. "You did so well, honey."

"Please untie me, Butterfly," he said.

She leaned forward. He moaned in disappointment when most of his cock slid out of her as she stretched for the restraints. She pulled the left one open and then the right and gasped in alarm when Max immediately sat up and grabbed her. Moving so quickly it made her head spin, he swung his legs over the side of the bed and slid forward until he was sitting on the side of it. He pulled her legs impatiently around his waist and held the back of her neck, pushing her down until she was filled completely with his cock.

"Max -"

He kissed with a desperate need, his other hand cupping her ass as he thrust. It was hard and deep and completely out of control and she clung to him as he kissed her and fucked her. He tore his mouth from hers, his entire body straining, and shouted hoarsely as he climaxed. He shoved his dick deep inside of her and shuddered helplessly. She rubbed his back and kissed his thick neck as he shook before collapsing on his back. He carried her with him, and she rested her head on his chest, listening to the harsh beat of his heart as he stroked her back.

"That seemed like a good one," she said.

"Best orgasm of my life," he rasped.

She laughed and patted him on the chest. "I bet you say that to all the girls."

"No," he said.

She lifted her head and studied him for a moment before stroking her hand across his beard. He kissed the palm of her hand and smiled at her and she curled up against him. They laid silently for a few minutes and, as doubt and guilt crept in, she touched his broad chest.

"What are we doing, Max?"

"If you don't know, then I'm not doing it right," he said with a low laugh.

She sat up and tugged the sheet around her body. "Be serious. We're just supposed to be friends, remember?"

"I guess we're friends with benefits now."

"Is that what you really want?" she said.

He hesitated and shook his head. "No."

She stared at her lap. "I can't give you what you want, Max."

"Why not?" he said. "Amanda, it's good between us – don't pretend you don't see that."

"You're one of my best friends and if we keep doing this, eventually I'll ruin everything."

"You don't know that."

"I do," she said.

"We can try. If it doesn't work, we'll still be friends."

"You know that isn't true. How many of your exes are you still friends with?"

"It's different with us, Amanda."

She sighed as hot tears pricked at her eyelids. "If I lose your friendship, Max, it'll be awful. Don't you see that? You're important to me and I can't throw that away just because you give me the best sex of my life."

He didn't reply and she took his hand and squeezed it. "I need to apologize for tonight. I deliberately tried to seduce you and I – I won't do that again, okay?"

"Right," he said bitterly.

She blinked back the tears. Already she had fucked up their friendship, she could see it in his face and hear it in his voice, and she swallowed down the panic that was rising in her throat. "Max, I'm sorry. I should never have crossed this line with you, and I -"

"Do you regret it?" he said. "Is that what you're going to tell me?"

"No, I don't regret it."

He threw back the covers and she grabbed at his arm. "Where are you going?"

"It's getting late. I should go home."

"You can stay the night," she said.

He laughed, that undercurrent of bitterness stronger now. "I'll do what you ask, Amanda. I'll go back to being just your friend, but don't deliberately torture me by asking me to sleep in your bed without being allowed to fuck you."

"I – that's not what I meant. I -"

"It's fine," he said. "Can you give me some space for a few days?"

Her heart dropped and she rubbed away the tears as he dressed. "Of course. I – I understand."

She scrubbed her face again as he finished dressing and glanced at her. "We're still friends, Amanda. I just need some time to clear my head."

"Okay," she said. She started to slide out of bed, and he shook his head.

"Stay in bed, I can show myself out. Good night, I'll text you in a few days."

"Good night, Max."

He left the bedroom and when she heard the front door shut, she burst into tears.

CHAPTER 8

Amanda left the locker room and headed for an empty treadmill. It was Sunday afternoon and she had moped around the house for the morning before packing up her gym stuff. Normally she met Max at the gym Sunday morning but, determined to give him his space, she waited until the afternoon. She didn't want to. She wanted to go at the same time she always did, wanted everything to be back to normal between them, but Max asked for time and she was going to give it to him.

Just because she needed reassurance that they were still friends didn't mean he was obligated to give it to her. She had done this in the past with boyfriends. A small disagreement or fight would put her into a tailspin of worry and anxiety over their relationship. Her constant badgering, her need to make sure that everything was still okay with them, would drive an even deeper wedge between them. She wouldn't do that with Max - she *couldn't* do that - so she had ignored her urge to text him to say hello and ignored the urge to go to the gym this morning. Everything would be fine with them. Max was a good guy and he said they were still friends. Everything would be *fine*.

"Amanda?"

She looked up, dismay crossing her face when she saw Max standing next to the full-length mirrors near the free weights. She took a step back, seriously considering turning and running back to the locker room.

"What are you doing here?" he said.

"I'm sorry," she said. "I – you normally go to the gym in the morning, so I waited until this afternoon but I…"

She folded her arms nervously across her torso. "I'm sorry, I'll leave."

"You don't have to leave. It's a big gym."

She bit her bottom lip. "Right. Okay, well, um, have a good workout, okay?"

"Thanks, you too."

He turned away, picking up two of the free weights and she hurried over to the treadmills. She climbed onto the closest one, turning it on and keeping her gaze on the bank of television screens mounted on the wall in front of her. She would do half an hour of cardio and then get her ass out of the gym.

MAX TOOK ANOTHER PEEK AT THE LINE OF TREADMILLS AS HE did his second set of curls. He groaned inwardly at the smooth flex of Amanda's ass as she walked. He had deliberately waited until this afternoon to go to the gym, not wanting to run into her this morning, but he should have known she would have done the same thing. He had asked for space and she was doing her best to give it to him, even though he had seen the fear in her eyes last night. She thought they had ruined their friendship.

Haven't you, though? You really think you can go back to being just friends?

Yes, he thought grimly. He could. He had to. Being with Amanda without touching her or taking her to his bed would be terrible, but a life without her at all was infinitely worse. He just needed a few days to get over his obsession with fucking her. A few days without seeing her would do the trick. He would forget the way her naked body looked and forget the sweet little moans she made when he touched her. The memory of sliding into the tightest, hottest pussy he'd ever felt would fade too.

You're an idiot.

No, he was just trying desperately to save a friendship that was very important to him.

You're in love with her and you think you can just be her friend. What happens when she starts dating someone? Will you be the supportive friend then?

She's done with relationships. She's not going to date anyone.

She's young and has a healthy appetite for sex. She won't be single forever.

Jealousy streaked through him. Fuck, his inner voice was right. Amanda was amazing in bed and now that her dry spell was over, she probably would be more interested in dating. Maybe he could convince her that he had changed his mind and was perfectly fine with a friends with benefits relationship. He would do it if it meant keeping other men away from her.

So, you're a pathetic idiot.

"Max – hi!"

He groaned inwardly before lowering the weights and

smiling at the woman who had appeared in front of him. "Hi, Gina. What, um, what are you doing here?"

"Well, after you told me how awesome your gym was on Friday night, I figured I'd try out a guest pass."

The slender, blue-haired girl studied his body before smiling up at him. "I didn't think I'd be so lucky to run into you."

He gave her an uncomfortable smile as she glanced around the gym. "Oh, hey, there's Amanda."

He followed her gaze as she waved excitedly. Her face pale, Amanda was staring at them as she walked on the treadmill. She raised her arm in a brief, choppy wave, before staring up at the television screens again.

"So," Gina smiled at him, "since we're both here, maybe you could show me some of those weight-lifting techniques you were talking about. I'm really wanting to build some muscle mass."

He hesitated before nodding. "Sure, I can do that."

"Great!" Gina said. "But first, I'm going to prove to you that I can do ten pull-ups. I know you didn't believe me. Come with me."

She took his hand and he glanced over his shoulder at Amanda. She was still staring at the televisions and Gina tugged at his hand impatiently. "Over here, Max."

He followed her to the bar, and she smiled at him. "Can you give me a boost?"

He put his hands around her waist and lifted her to the bar. She adjusted her grip before winking at him. "Be prepared to be amazed, Max Westman."

Stop looking over there, Amanda. Are you deliberately trying to torture yourself?

She wasn't, at least she didn't think she was, but she took another peek anyway. Jealousy flooded through her when Max put his hands around Gina's waist and lifted her to the pull-up bar. As Gina began to do an impressive number of pull-ups, she cursed inwardly. While she'd always thought her body was good, Gina had an amazing body. Her abs were clearly defined and absolutely nothing jiggled on her.

Max would love that, she thought as a wave of depression washed over her. He was big into fitness and while she didn't mind going to the gym and was, surprisingly, even starting to enjoy it a little she would never be like Gina.

Max doesn't like Gina. He told you that.

Yes, he had. But that was when he thought there was a chance for something between them. Now that she had rejected him, had made it perfectly clear that they would only every be friends, why wouldn't Max try dating Gina? He was lonely and he wanted to be in a relationship. He and Gina would make a cute couple.

Her stomach cramped painfully, and she abruptly stopped the treadmill as Gina dropped to the floor and smiled at Max. She flexed her arm, pointing to it, and laughed when Max squeezed her bicep obligingly.

Amanda hurriedly wiped down the treadmill before scurrying toward the locker room. She couldn't stay here a minute longer and watch Gina flirt with Max. Keeping her head down, she prayed silently that Max and Gina wouldn't notice her leaving.

"Amanda! Hey, Amanda!"

She groaned and forced her head up, keeping her body moving briskly as she smiled at Gina.

"Come over and visit for a minute," Gina called.

"Sorry, I can't!" Amanda said. "I'm already running late. Have a great workout, you two!"

She waved at the both of them, her grin widening until she thought her face would crack in two, and hurried into the locker room. The smile dropped from her face and she ran to her locker, opening it and stuffing her clothes into her gym bag. If Max started dating Gina, she would support them and be genuinely happy for them. Well, maybe not genuinely happy but she would fake it really well. Max deserved to have a woman who loved him and wouldn't break his heart.

You love him.

She staggered to a stop, staring blankly at the lime green walls of the locker room. Okay, so she loved him, but she had loved boyfriends in the past and look how that had turned out.

Max is different.

Yes, he was. He wasn't a bad boy, he was a good man who would treat her well, and maybe it would take longer than usual for her personality to start to grate on him. But when it did – when he finally couldn't take her compulsive need to be with him all the time, the way she would expect him to drop everything for her whenever she needed him – and he ended their relationship, it would destroy her. It was better to have him as her friend than to not have him at all.

"Hello, Lucy."

"Hey, Max. How was your weekend?"

"It was good. How was yours?" He dropped into the chair beside her desk.

"Good."

"I didn't see you at the staff meeting this morning," he said.

"I had an appointment." Lucy studied him for a moment. "Is everything okay?"

"Yes, why wouldn't it be?"

"You look upset."

"I'm not," he said.

"Everything okay with Amanda?" Lucy asked.

"Did she say it wasn't?"

Lucy shook her head. "No, but I haven't talked to her since lunch on Saturday."

"You know we had sex, don't you?"

"Yes, Amanda told me."

He slumped in his chair and rubbed at his forehead. "I went over to her place Saturday night for dinner, and I told myself that I would just be her friend but I – I couldn't keep my hands off of her. We had sex again."

Lucy gave him a cautious look. "Well, you two have a lot of chemistry and I don't think it's a bad thing if you try dating."

He shook his head. "Immediately after, Amanda told me we couldn't do it again. That my friendship was too important to her and she didn't want to lose it. Only, I know that's not the reason. She likes bad boys and I'm too nice for her. I never thought being nice to a woman would work against me."

Lucy stared at him sympathetically. "I'm sorry, Max. Amanda is – well, she's afraid of hurting you. I don't think she's ever had a healthy relationship before and all those stupid bad boys she's dated have coloured her view of herself. She blames herself every time something goes wrong, thinks she's too clingy and needy because those assholes convinced her she was."

"She isn't," Max said. "She's strong and independent and

so damn sweet and funny. Hell, sometimes I wish she needed me more."

"You're in love with her, aren't you," Lucy said.

"Yeah, I am. How's that for stupid?"

"It's not stupid."

"It is," he said. "She doesn't love me – at least not the way that I love her."

"Are you sure?"

"Yeah. If she did, she wouldn't have pushed me away. She wouldn't be insisting that we just be friends."

"I think she's afraid," Lucy said. "Maybe if you talked to her again, she would -"

"No," Max said. "She made it perfectly clear what she wanted Saturday night and I agreed to it. I asked her for a few days to clear my head, and she's giving it to me. We ran into each other at the gym on Sunday and she – she looked terrified that I was going to, I don't know, yell at her or something for not giving me space."

He rubbed again at his forehead. "The stupid thing is, I asked her to give me some space and now I miss her so much, it's pathetic. It's been less than twenty-four hours since I saw her, and I keep wanting to text her or call or drop by her place."

"Then do it," Lucy said.

"I can't. Right now, I'd try to have sex with her again and she doesn't want that. I won't do that to her, Luce."

"I'm sorry, Max."

"Yeah, me too," he said.

"I could try to talk to her, if you want," Lucy said.

"No, that's okay. I don't want to drag you into the middle of this."

"I don't mind. Amanda is my best friend and maybe I can

talk some sense into her. She should be with you, Max, she just doesn't realize it yet."

He smiled at her. "Thanks, but it's okay."

"Well, if you change your mind, let me know," Lucy said. Her cell phone rang, and she grabbed it off her desk. Her face paled.

"Everything okay?" Max said.

"Yeah, I need to take this."

He stood and headed for the door. "Thanks, Luce. I'll talk to you later."

"Sure. Can you close the door on the way out?"

He closed the door, and she took a deep breath as she stared at the doctor's number. This morning at her appointment, after listening to her symptoms, Dr. Flint had insisted on doing a pregnancy test along with other blood tests. He was as skeptical as she was about the possibility of her being pregnant, but it hadn't stopped him from sending her to the in-clinic lab. He had told her they would have the results either later this afternoon or tomorrow morning and, taking another deep breath, she answered her cell phone.

Five minutes later, she set her cell phone on the desk and stared at her hands. They were shaking wildly, and, after a moment, she covered her face with her trembling hands and sobbed.

"LUCY? WHAT'S GOING ON?" JASON SMILED DISTRACTEDLY at the nurse who showed him into the room before hurrying to the exam table. Lucy was perched on it and wearing a hospital gown. She smiled at him.

"Were you able to reschedule your meeting? I'm sorry, I

know it was short notice for you to come here but I wanted you here for this."

"Yeah, it wasn't an issue. Here for what?" Jason stared at her in bewilderment.

She took his hands and squeezed them. "You know how I haven't been feeling well, right?"

"Yeah, bad Thai food."

"Right," she said with a small smile. "The vomiting wasn't getting better and, I didn't tell you this, but I've missed my period for the last three months. This morning I made an appointment with Dr. Flint."

Jason's face paled. "Is the infection back? I thought the antibiotics would clear it up."

"They did," she said. "It's not an infection."

"Then why are we here?" he said. "Why are you wearing a hospital gown?"

"Dr. Flint did a few blood tests this morning," she said. "Including a pregnancy test."

"Why would he do that? He said that you couldn't get pregnant," Jason said.

"He said there was a less than five percent chance I could get pregnant," she said. Tears started to slide down her cheeks as a brief look of hope crossed Jason's face.

"Lucy, are you…"

She smiled at him as more tears flowed down her face. "I'm pregnant. We beat the odds, Jason."

"You're pregnant," he repeated.

"Yes. About twelve weeks," she said. "It must have happened while we were on our honeymoon."

"You're pregnant," he whispered.

She nodded again and burst into tears when Jason made a whoop of delight and wrapped his arms around her waist. He lifted her off the exam table and twirled her around as she laughed and hugged him.

"Jason, put me down. You'll put your back out."

He set her on the exam table and kissed her. "I love you, Lucy."

"I love you too."

He squeezed her thighs with his warm hands. "Why are we here though?"

"Dr. Flint asked me to come back so he could do an ultrasound. He wants to make sure that the baby is healthy and everything is normal."

"Is he worried that it's an ectopic pregnancy?" Jason asked.

"Yes," she said.

There was a knock at the door and Dr. Flint walked into the room. "Ready to go, Lucy? Hello, Jason."

"Hi, Dr. Flint," Jason said as Lucy nodded.

"Good. Lay back and lift your gown and we'll get started. Jason, why don't you stand here at Lucy's head. That way you can both see the screen."

Jason held Lucy's hand as Dr. Flint squeezed gel onto the ultrasound wand.

"This will be cold," Dr. Flint warned before gliding the wand over Lucy's stomach. Her hand tightened on Jason's and he leaned down and kissed her forehead. They waited in tense anticipation as Dr. Flint moved the wand in a gentle back and forth motion.

Lucy's heart thudded heavily as Dr. Flint suddenly smiled and adjusted the volume. There was a muffled sounding rhythmic beat, light and quick, and Dr. Flint smiled again. "That's your baby's heartbeat."

Lucy started to cry, and Jason kissed her again as Dr. Flint pointed to the screen. "And there's your baby."

They stared at the screen as Dr. Flint said, "That's the head, obviously, and there's a foot."

"Is it – I mean, is the baby in the right spot?" Jason said.

Dr. Flint nodded. "Yes. This is looking like a healthy, normal pregnancy. Congratulations."

He reached out and turned the screen away. "Baby's turning. Do you want to know the sex?"

Lucy glanced at Jason and he shook his head. "I'd rather it be a surprise."

"Me too," she said.

"No problem," Dr. Flint said. "Honestly, I wouldn't be confident that I was right, anyway. I'll book you in at the hospital for a regular twelve-week ultrasound with a sonographer within the next week or so. They'll check baby's growth and organs and look for any abnormalities. Okay?"

"Okay," Lucy said.

Jason rested his forehead against Lucy's and kissed her before wiping the tears from her cheeks. "We're having a baby."

She laughed through her tears. "Yes, we are."

AMANDA STARED IN STUNNED SILENCE AT LUCY AND JASON. "You're having a baby," she said.

Lucy grinned at her. "We are."

"I have super sperm, apparently," Jason said.

Lucy laughed and whacked him on the chest. "The doctor did not say you have super sperm, Jason Young."

"No, but we both know I do," he said.

"You're having a baby," Amanda repeated.

"Yes," Lucy said.

"Holy shit!" Amanda screamed and yanked Lucy into her

arms. She hugged her before hugging Jason and then hugging Lucy again. "You're pregnant! Oh, honey, I'm so happy for you guys!"

"Thanks, Amanda," Lucy said.

"Take Amanda out on to the deck while I grab the wine for us and the sparkling water for you," Jason said.

Lucy took Amanda's hand and led her out onto the small deck. They sat on the futon as Lenny wandered out after them and jumped into Lucy's lap. She petted him as Amanda squeezed her leg.

"How far along are you?"

"About three months. I have an appointment on Friday at the hospital for an ultrasound. They'll check everything out, but Dr. Flint did an ultrasound yesterday afternoon and he thinks everything looks normal."

"Oh, honey," Amanda said, "I can't believe it."

"You and me both," Lucy said. "But all the vomiting I've been doing assures me that it's really happening."

"Have you told anyone else yet?"

Lucy shook her head as Jason joined them on the deck. He handed a glass to Lucy before giving Amanda her wine glass.

"We thought we would wait until after the ultrasound on Friday," Jason said. "Make sure everything is good before we tell our families."

He sat down beside Lucy on the futon and the three of them watched the sun slowly set over the waves.

"We'll have to get a new place," Jason said.

"I guess," Lucy replied. "But not right away. The den is big enough for a nursery."

"Do you know what you're having?" Amanda asked.

"No. We want it to be a surprise. I'll need your help decorating the nursery in neutral colours," Lucy said.

"Of course." Amanda sipped at her wine. For the first time since Max had left her bed Saturday night, she was truly happy, and she smiled at Lucy as Jason's cell phone buzzed.

He checked it and sent off a quick text. "That was Max. He's still at the office."

"Still?" Lucy said.

"Yeah. He discovered some problems with the financials that Maureen did last year, and it's totally fucked up all of his numbers. It's actually a real mess and he was nearly tearing out his hair earlier this afternoon over it. But he thinks he's figured out how to fix it."

He took a sip of wine. "Thank God. We'd be fucked if he couldn't fix it. Of course, it'll probably take weeks for him to get it all sorted out."

"Poor guy," Lucy said.

"Yeah. He's in for a hellish few weeks," Jason replied before glancing at Amanda. "Don't be surprised if he doesn't have time to hang out for a while."

Amanda finished her wine in two large gulps. She wouldn't be seeing Max anyway, at least not until he decided if he really could just be friends with her. But at least if it went on for a while, she could comfort herself by pretending it was because he was busy at work.

"More wine?" Jason asked.

"Yes. I think a second glass of wine is an appropriate way to celebrate you becoming parents."

He laughed and took her glass before disappearing into the house. Lucy grabbed her hand and squeezed it. "Have you and Max made up yet?"

"I haven't talked to him since Sunday when we ran into each other at the gym."

"I'm sorry," Lucy said.

"It's fine," Amanda forced herself to sound cheerful.

"We're not fighting or anything, he needs some space and I understand that. I should never have slept with him, I know that now, but all I can do at this point is damage control. Hopefully, he'll miss my friendship as much as I miss his and we can start hanging out again."

"Maybe you should call him."

"No," Amanda said. "I won't be like I usually am and act like a needy, spoiled brat. He's asked me for space and I'm going to give it to him. Besides, it sounds like he's going to be pretty busy at work anyway."

"Amanda -"

"Tonight isn't about me," Amanda said. "Tonight is about you and Jason and your baby. Let's talk more about this nursery. Do we have a theme or what?"

Lucy shrugged. "I haven't really thought that far ahead."

"Well, let's figure it out tonight. It'll be fun," Amanda said. "Also, keep in mind that Amanda is a beautiful name for a girl."

Lucy laughed and Amanda leaned forward and hugged her again before whispering, "I'm so happy for you, Lucy. I love you."

"Thanks, honey. I love you too."

CHAPTER 9

This is a bad idea, Amanda.

She ignored her inner voice as she lifted the basket from her car and walked up the sidewalk to Max's house. It wasn't a bad idea. She had thought all day about Max and after work she had hit up a few places and made a care package for him. The basket was filled with some of his favourite snacks and a few gift cards to his favourite restaurants. He would probably be working lots of overtime over the next week or so, and she was worried that he wouldn't have time to cook.

It was close to seven, but she had done a drive-by first to make sure he wasn't home. His truck wasn't parked in its normal spot on the street and the blinds on his house had all been closed. She climbed the front steps and set the basket in front of the door. She had a key to Max's house, just like he had one to hers, but it didn't feel right to her to invade his space. Not after he had made it clear he didn't want her around him right now.

She hesitated before sliding the card from the envelope and reading it again.

. . .

Max,

I heard you were working some long hours. Hope this helps!

Amanda

THAT SOUNDED OKAY, SHE DECIDED. LEAVING A CARE package was something a friend would do, and the note was friendly but not desperate sounding or anything. She slid the card back into the envelope and tucked it neatly into the top of the basket.

"What are you doing here?"

She screamed at the sound of Max's voice and jerked before tripping and falling off the cement stoop. She landed in the bushes in front of his house, cursing when she scraped her bare knee, and scrambled to tug down her skirt.

"Shit! Amanda, are you okay?" Max reached for her and she scooted backward on her butt before struggling to her feet. She smiled at him as blood dripped down her leg.

"Max, uh, hi."

"Are you okay?"

"Yes, fine. I'm sorry, I didn't think you would be home yet. I saw Lucy last night and she, um, told me you'd be working some long hours so I thought that I would leave a little, uh, care package for you."

She pointed to the basket and Max glanced at it before staring at her again. She blushed furiously at the look on his face. "I'm sorry. It was a stupid idea."

"It wasn't," he said.

"Right. Well, I have to go. I'm sorry for flattening your bushes. I'll buy you some new ones."

She hesitated for a moment - it had been three days since she'd seen him at the gym and she missed him terribly – before slipping around his big body. She ignored her urge to throw her arms around him and hug him and instead, limped down the sidewalk.

"Amanda, wait."

She froze and chewed on her bottom lip before plastering a smile on her face and turning to face Max.

"You're bleeding," he said.

"It's only a scrape. I'll slap a bandage on it when I get home. Goodnight, Max."

"Come inside. We can bandage it here, so you don't get blood all over your car."

"No, no," she said. "I have some tissue in my purse. It's fine, really."

"Come inside, Amanda," he said.

She didn't move and he scowled at her before picking up the basket and unlocking the front door. "Come inside, I said."

Sighing, she limped up the sidewalk and into his house.

"Sorry," Max grunted when she hissed in pain.

"It's fine," she said.

He sprayed some more antibiotic spray on the scrape before placing a piece of gauze on it and taping it with medical tape. She tried not to shiver at the touch of his warm hands and failed miserably.

His hand cupped her calf for a minute before he stood and gathered up the garbage. "All done," he said.

"Thanks, Max."

"You're welcome. Thankfully, I only faint at the sight of

my own blood," he said. "And, thanks for the care package, it was a really nice gesture."

She gave him a tentative smile. "It isn't much, but I thought it might help a little since you're so busy at work."

She studied him as he threw away the garbage. He looked tired and out-of-sorts and he rubbed absentmindedly at his beard. He gave her a weird look, and she realized that she was sitting at the table and staring at him like an idiot. She blushed and stood. He had asked for his space and here she was, sitting in his kitchen and wishing that he would kiss her already, even though she knew he was tired and grumpy and didn't want anything to do with her.

"I'm going to go," she said. "Sorry again. I hope your week goes smoothly."

She wanted to ask him when he thought he might be ready to be friends again, but she bit her tongue and plastered another smile on her face. She would not be a whiny, needy baby. She absolutely would not.

"Bye, Max!" She hurried for the door.

His big hand was wrapping around her arm before she was even out of the kitchen and she gasped when he pushed her against the wall.

He held her immobile with one hard hand against her stomach – fuck it should not turn her on so much to have him touching her - and stared at her. "Why are you really here, Amanda?"

"I – I told you," she said. "I knew you were working some late hours and thought a care package would be a nice thing to do. I didn't think you would be home so soon, or I wouldn't have come by. I swear."

"A care package," he said almost angrily. "You came by because you thought I needed a care package."

"Yes," she whispered.

He leaned down, his warm breath washing over her, and she stifled her moan of need as he said, "You sure you didn't come by because you've got an itch you need scratching?"

She stared wide-eyed at him as his hand tightened on her abdomen. "Is that it? You want me to scratch your itch, Butterfly?"

"No, of course not," she whispered but oh, it sounded like a lie – even to her.

She cleared her throat. "The package has some gift cards to your favourite restaurants and some snacks. I know it's going to be busy at work and I wanted to do something nice for you, that's all. I wanted to make you, uh, feel better."

His other hand curled into her hair and this time she couldn't stop the moan when he pulled her head back and lowered his mouth to her throat. He nipped her hard and she flattened her hands against the wall to stop from sliding them around his waist.

"Max, I should go," she whispered.

"What if I told you that your pretty little mouth sucking my dick would make me feel better?" he said into her ear.

She made another harsh moan, desire rushing through her as an embarrassing amount of liquid gushed from her pussy.

"Is sucking my cock part of your care package, Butterfly?"

She stared up at him before nodding. "If that's what you want."

He didn't reply and she pulled his hand away from her hair before kneeling in front of him. She winced at the pain in her scraped knee when it touched the hard tile but reached for the front of his pants.

He hauled her to her feet, and she stared at him. "Max, please. I want to do this for you."

"Your knee," he said hoarsely.

"It's fine. Let me -"

He shook his head and took her by the arm. She wanted to cry with disappointment. He was going to make her leave and she wanted him so desperately. Her pulse sped up when instead of leading her toward the front door, he turned left and headed to his bedroom. He opened the door and nearly jerked her into the room before picking her up and sitting her on the side of the bed. She had never been in his bedroom before, and she stared wide-eyed at the bed. It was massive, over seven feet long and so high her feet didn't touch the floor.

Her gaze snapped forward when she heard the rasp of Max's zipper. He had already removed his shirt and he pushed her legs apart with his thighs and stood in front of her. His crotch was directly in front of her and, shamefully, her mouth began to water when he shoved down his pants and briefs. She stared at his cock as, without speaking, he cupped the back of her head and pulled her toward it. She opened her mouth and sucked eagerly at his dick when he pushed it past her lips. He held her hair as he thrust back and forth. His low groans sent lust rocketing through her and she sucked frantically as he rocked back and forth.

The head of his cock hit the back of her throat and she tried to control her gag reflex. He pulled out and petted her hair, brushing it back from her face. "Sorry, Butterfly."

"It's okay," she said and grabbed the base of his cock. She stroked the base as she sucked and licked at his cock and he moaned and fisted his hands in her hair. She stared up at him as she sucked, and he smiled and brushed her hair back again.

"Such a good girl, Butterfly," he said.

She sucked him harder in response and he groaned before letting his head fall back and thrusting roughly back and forth. She licked around the ridge before sliding her tongue along the thick vein on the underside. He shuddered all over before his hands tightened almost painfully in her hair.

"Amanda, wait," he said.

She shook her head and attacked his cock with renewed vigor. She wanted to make him feel good, wanted to do something to make up for how badly she kept fucking things up with him. If this was what he needed, she was more than happy to do it. Besides, sucking his dick was apparently a huge turn on for her. She was fairly certain she had soaked through her panties and was currently ruining her skirt.

After he comes and then makes you leave, what do you think his neighbours will say when they see the big wet spot on your skirt?

She didn't care. All she cared about was making Max feel good. He wouldn't fuck her but as soon as he was taken care of, she'd drive home in record time and have a nice long visit with her vibrator. She had an active imagination – she could pretend it was Max fucking her.

She whimpered pathetically when he pulled away from her. Panting, she gave him a pleading look as he grabbed her waist.

"Please let me finish," she said.

He shook his head and she squealed in surprise when he flipped her over. "Hands and knees and don't move," he demanded.

She balanced on her hands and knees. The bed was soft, she barely felt the throb of her scraped knee, and she clutched at the quilt as her pulse thudded heavily. She heard the sound of the foil from the condom and when Max shoved up her skirt and tore her panties from her body, she moaned in anticipation.

His hands spread her thighs wide, and he held her by the shoulder as he guided his cock to her pussy. He was frustrated with her and she tensed a little. He wouldn't be gentle, but she was soaking wet and she just needed to remember to breathe.

His hand rubbed her bare ass as he rumbled, "You're tense. Why?"

"I'm not," she lied.

"You are," he said before stroking her thighs. "I'll never hurt you, Amanda."

"I know," she said. "Fuck me, Max."

He rubbed her ass again, his other hand kneading the back of her neck until she relaxed. To her surprise, he didn't thrust roughly into her. He was as slow and gentle as he always was, taking his time despite his frustration, and she pushed back against him when he withdrew.

"There's my greedy girl," he said with a low laugh. "Have you missed my cock, Butterfly?"

She looked over her shoulder at him. "I've missed you."

"I've missed you too," he said. Holding her gaze, he pushed steadily forward until he was fully encased in her wet, tight warmth. He moved back and forth, and she continued to stare at him until he leaned forward and slipped his hands under her body. He yanked her shirt open, tearing off the buttons and ripping the delicate fabric, before pulling it over her head and down her arms. He flicked open the clasp on her bra, shoving it down her arms and leaving it and her ruined shirt tangled around her wrists as he cupped both of her breasts.

She arched her back, filling his hands with her small breasts, and he tugged on her nipples before licking up her spine. She cried out, her hands clenching around the quilt and he kissed both her shoulder blades before cupping her throat. Holding her firmly, he stroked back and forth, each thick glide of his cock brushing against the front wall of her pussy and making her moan. When his fingers rubbed her clit, she screamed and came immediately, her body writhing in his grip as a tidal wave of pleasure washed through her. He groaned under his breath and fucked her hard, each thrust driving into her as she struggled to keep her balance. He pushed on her lower back and she lowered her upper body to the bed, resting her heated cheek on the quilt, as he pounded in and out of her.

She could feel another orgasm starting and she rocked her hips back and forth, silently begging him to fuck her harder. He shoved her thighs further apart and buried himself deep inside of her. She could hear him panting, each exhale a low moan that made her shiver with pleasure. When his fingers bit into the milky flesh of her hips, she closed her eyes and whispered his name as she climaxed again. He shouted hoarsely, his body stiffening as he came. She squeezed around him, holding him deep inside of her until his grip relaxed on her hips.

He pulled out and she collapsed on the bed, her hair sticking to her sweaty face and her chest heaving as she panted for air. He disposed of the condom before lying down beside her. She wanted to curl into him, wanted to rest her head on his chest, but she resisted. This wasn't anything more than a stress release for Max and she totally understood that. She wouldn't embarrass herself by trying to cuddle with him. In fact, she should get dressed and leave.

She pulled off her bra and ruined shirt and started to sit up. Max immediately pulled her into his embrace. She slung her arm around his waist and kissed his broad chest before resting her cheek against it. She would give herself fifteen minutes to enjoy cuddling him and then she would leave.

"Feel better?" she asked.

"Much," he replied.

"Good," she said. "I'm sorry work has been such a nightmare."

He shrugged and they relaxed in silence, his hand stroking her back lazily as she rubbed his flat abdomen.

When her fifteen minutes were up, she forced herself to sit up. She smiled down at him before patting his chest. "Can I borrow a shirt? I'll wash it and drop it by your house before you're done work tomorrow."

He stared at her ripped shirt. "I'm sorry. I'll replace this one."

She shook her head. "You don't have to do that. I, um, I'd better go."

"Why?" he said.

"Well, because I want to give you your space," she said. "When I came by tonight it was because I really thought you wouldn't be home yet."

She stared earnestly at him. "I swear I didn't come over here to trick you into having sex with me, Max."

"I know you didn't," he said.

She slid off the bed and pulled on her skirt and bra before grabbing a t-shirt from his closet and slipping it over her head. She smiled at how big it was on her before tossing her shirt and panties into the garbage in the bathroom.

Max was still lying on his back on the bed and staring at the ceiling. She leaned over and pressed a kiss on his forehead. "Bye, Max."

"I want to be friends with benefits," he said.

She stared cautiously at him. "What?"

"Friends with benefits. I know you don't want to date me, but I've thought it over and I'm good with being friends with benefits."

"It isn't that I don't want to date you. I don't want to hurt you," she said.

"Whatever, Amanda. Do you want to be friends with benefits or not?" he said in frustration.

"You don't want that, Max."

"So now you can read my mind?" he snapped. "I said I was good with it so let's leave it at that. If you want sex, let me know and if I want sex, I'll let you know. When either one of us starts an actual relationship, we'll go back to being just friends."

She wanted to argue with him, but that tired, pinched look was back on his face and she knew instinctively that now was not the time. Instead, she pressed another kiss on his forehead and said, "We'll talk about it later, okay?"

"Yeah, sure," he said in defeat.

She squeezed his shoulder and forced herself to walk out of his bedroom.

MAX STARED AT THE CEILING BEFORE CURSING. WHEN HE HAD come home from work to find Amanda standing on his doorstep it had taken all of his willpower to not simply pick her up and carry her into his bedroom. He hadn't seen or talked to her since Sunday and the last three days had been horrible. Forgetting the fucking nightmare that work was at the moment, he missed Amanda so much his entire body was aching.

He hated that she had hurt herself but was selfishly glad that it gave him an excuse to bring her inside. He had honestly meant to just bandage her up and talk to her about the friends with benefits thing but then he had lost his goddamn mind and went all caveman on her.

She didn't seem to mind.

He rolled over to his side and stared blankly at the wall.

No, she hadn't, thank God, but she certainly was in a hurry to leave.

Because you told her you wanted space.

He sat up and threw on a pair of shorts before heading to the kitchen. Yeah, he told her that and he had never regretted anything more. Well, except for telling her he wanted to be friends with benefits. She hadn't said no but she hadn't agreed to it either. He shouldn't have done that, but he was feeling pathetically desperate for her. An almost overwhelming wave of panic went through him. If she didn't agree to at least being friends with benefits, he'd have to end their friendship. He couldn't see her without touching her or kissing her.

He grabbed a beer from the fridge before rifling through the basket Amanda had brought. A small smile crossed his face, and he tore open the package of caramel cakes and popped one into his mouth. God, she was so sweet and thoughtful. He couldn't imagine his life without her.

He took a long swallow of beer and stared moodily out the window of the kitchen. He would give her a couple of days to think about what he said. She had to say yes, she had to.

———

THURSDAY AFTERNOON, AMANDA WAS REORGANIZING THE bottles of product on the shelves in the salon when Gina came skipping out from the back room. She stood behind the desk and grinned happily at Angie.

"What's got you in such a good mood?" Angie asked.

"Max texted me and agreed to have drinks with me tonight," Gina said as she tucked her cell phone into her pocket. She and Angie both jumped at the loud clatter and turned to see Amanda, bottles of shampoo and conditioner scattered at her feet, staring wide-eyed at them.

"Amanda? What's wrong?" Angie asked.

Amanda shook her head before bending over and picking up the bottles she had dropped. "Nothing."

She placed the bottles on the shelves, staring numbly at them as Angie said, "So, where are you and Max going for drinks?"

"Josie's Bar and Pub. It's going to be a bit later, Max said he's really busy at work right now, but that will give me time to go home and change and make myself look irresistible."

Angie laughed, "You thinking it might end up being more than just drinks?"

"Maybe," Gina replied with a coy grin. "Max said he's been working late all week so I might suggest he comes back to my place for a relaxing back rub. If that turns into something more…well, I'm not going to complain."

"You go, girl," Angie said. She frowned when Amanda slipped past her. "Are you okay, Amanda? You're pale."

"Fine," Amanda said. "I need to use the bathroom before my next appointment."

She hurried into the back room and bolted for the bathroom. She locked the door and stared at herself in the mirror. She felt sick to her stomach and for a moment she thought she might vomit.

Get it together, Amanda!

She bent over and took five big breaths, concentrating on inhaling and exhaling, before straightening and gripping the sink. Max was going on a date with Gina, and she couldn't do a thing about it. He had asked to be friends with benefits, and she hadn't agreed to it and now it was too late. He was seeing someone else. Why the hell hadn't she said yes right away last night?

You didn't think he would start dating Gina, that's why. He had sex with you last night and now he's going out with another woman. Maybe Max isn't the good guy you think he is.

She shook her head. No, Max was a good guy. They hadn't made any promises to each other and she wouldn't even agree to just friends with benefits. She had no right to be upset that he had decided to date Gina. She bit back her sobs and blinked rapidly. She would not cry at work. Max deserved happiness and if Gina made him happy then, goddammit, she would be happy for him.

You're such a moron. You ruined your chance with Max because you're too stupid and too afraid to admit that you love him.

She tightened her hands around the sink, staring bleakly at the pale-faced version of herself in the mirror, and whispered, "Shut up! Just shut up!"

Her inner voice wisely shut up. After a moment, she washed her hands and pinched some colour back into her cheeks before returning to her station.

CHAPTER 10

Max stood and stretched before walking to the window of his office and staring down at the traffic. It was almost lunch on Friday and his stomach rumbled. He grabbed the box of caramel cakes he had brought from Amanda's care package and ate one before downing the cold coffee that was left in his mug.

He stared at the spreadsheet on his computer screen before turning to face the window again. He had come in early this morning because he didn't want to work late tonight. He yawned before scrubbing his hand over his beard. It'd been a late night last night. Gina had been texting him all week and he finally agreed to meet with her for drinks. He supposed he could have told her by text that he only wanted to be her friend but that seemed like a shitty thing to do to her. He met Gina for drinks around nine and told her that he wasn't interested, and would never be interested, in being anything more than friends. She was disappointed but not terribly upset by the news, and they'd had a drink and chatted for an hour or so.

It was close to eleven by the time he had climbed into

bed. Exhausted, he had lain awake for another two hours thinking about Amanda. He finally decided to talk to her today - he needed to know where they stood with each other - and that decision had allowed his mind to calm the fuck down so he could get some sleep.

He glanced at his watch when his stomach rumbled again before striding toward the door. He would drop by the salon and see if Amanda wanted to have lunch. He couldn't go the afternoon without knowing what her decision was and if she did agree to his proposal, then maybe they could make plans to hang out tonight.

Have sex, you mean.

He ignored the disapproval in his inner voice as he headed toward the elevator. Having sex was what friends with benefits did. That was the whole damn point.

"SO, DO YOU THINK GINA'S ACTUALLY SICK TODAY OR DO you think she spent the night having crazy hot sex with Max and now she can't walk?" Angie asked Amanda.

Amanda forced a smile to her face. "I don't know."

"My vote is for the crazy hot sex. Max is huge and Gina is so tiny that there's no way she was walking normal after being in his bed."

Amanda didn't reply and Angie cocked an eyebrow at her. "Max didn't say anything to you about last night? You two are, like, best friends."

"We don't talk about our sex lives," Amanda said.

"Is there something wrong?" Angie asked.

"No. Of course not," Amanda said. "It's almost lunch. Why don't you take your break first? I'll watch phones."

"Sure," Angie said. "I have to run to the bank and then

I'm going to grab a sandwich. Do you want me to pick you up something?"

"No, I'm not hungry," Amanda said. "Thanks though."

She tidied up her station as Angie grabbed her coat and her jacket and left. When Angie was gone, Amanda sat in the chair behind reception and buried her face in her hands. She didn't know what was worse – Gina being at work and having to hear all the details of her date with Max, or Gina not being here and having her imagination going crazy. Maybe Gina called in sick because she was still with Max. Maybe she was in Max's bed right now and he was touching her and kissing her and calling her butterfly in that low voice of his.

Jealousy made her stomach cramp and she winced and rubbed at it as bile rose in her throat. Max and Gina weren't together right now. Max was busy at work and he wasn't the kind of guy to call in sick for a day of sex. He was responsible and –

"Amanda?"

She glanced up, her mouth dropping open and the colour fading from her cheeks. She stood and stumbled back a few steps. "What are you doing here?"

"I just want to talk, okay?"

"Get out, Jamie," she said. "I have nothing to say to you."

"Please, Amanda. Hear me out, will you?" Jamie pleaded.

He looked different. His hair was cut short, and he was clean-shaven. Instead of his usual ripped jeans and faded t-shirt, he was wearing a clean pair of jeans and a dress shirt.

"You need to leave," she said again. She took a nervous look around the salon. She was alone and if Jamie lost his temper...

"I want to apologize," Jamie said.

She laughed bitterly. "Yeah, right."

163

She circled around the desk and headed for the front door, stiffening when Jamie grabbed her arm as she walked by him.

"No, I do," he said. "I know how shitty I treated you, Amanda."

"It was beyond shitty," she said. "Now let go of me before I punch you in the face."

To her surprise he let go immediately and took a step back, holding up his hands. "Please, Amanda. Five minutes, that's all I'm asking, and then I'll leave and never come near you again."

She studied him suspiciously before nodding. "Five minutes, not a second more."

"Thank you," he said. He hesitated and she glanced at the clock on the wall above the reception desk. He gave her a faint smile. "Sorry, I'm trying to think of how to start."

She didn't reply and he studied his hands for a moment before smiling again at her. "I was an alcoholic and drug addict. It was starting to get pretty bad before I moved to New York, although I still had some control over it, but once I was in the city, I pretty much lost it. All I cared about was drinking and getting high and I – I did some pretty awful things to you and other people who cared about me."

She stared wide-eyed at him as he continued. "About two months ago, my dad came to New York and he gave me a choice. He said I could go to rehab and get clean, or he was cutting me out of the family. He and my mom would – would stop loaning me money, I wouldn't be allowed in their home, and they would stop speaking to me. It scared me, Amanda. Until that moment, I knew that no matter how much I fucked up, my mom and dad would always be there. Knowing that they wouldn't be – it scared me enough for me to agree to go to rehab."

He wiped hands nervously on his pants before raising his

gaze to hers again. "I'm clean now. Fifty-eight days sober today."

"Congratulations," she said.

"Thanks."

"Have you moved back here?" she said.

"No, not yet anyway. I might eventually but for now I'm going to be living at an outpatient rehab facility. I can stay there for up to a year so that'll give me some time to figure out what I want to do with my life."

He took a step toward her. "Dr. Minch, that's my therapist at rehab, talked to me a lot about making amends, about apologizing to the people I had hurt when I was drinking and getting high. In therapy I made a list of people I needed to ask forgiveness for and you're on that list, Amanda, right after my parents."

He took a deep breath and stared solemnly at her. "I'm so sorry, Amanda. I'm sorry for the horrible things I said to you, for the terrible way I treated you and for dragging you into my fucked-up life. The things I said weren't true. I accused you of being clingy and being needy when, in reality, you were being a good person and I didn't know how to deal with that. I lied to you, I cheated on you, and I said hurtful things that weren't true. I am truly sorry for doing that to you. I know I don't deserve your forgiveness but I'm asking for it anyway. If there's anything I can do to make up for the things I said and did, I'll do it."

She stared silently at him and he said, "I know it's a lot to ask and I understand if you never want to see or hear from me again. I'm in town for a couple more days. I'm staying with my parents and if you want to get together and maybe have a cup of coffee, I'd like that. You can call their home number. It was good to see you again, Amanda. I'm so sorry for the way I treated you."

He turned to leave and Amanda, her throat burning, said, "Jamie?"

"Yeah?"

"I forgive you."

His chin quivered and he looked down at the floor before saying huskily, "Just like that, huh?"

"Just like that."

He stared at her, blinking back tears before clearing his throat. "Thank you, Amanda. That means a lot to me. Could I – would it be okay if I hugged you?"

"Yes."

He hugged her and she rubbed his back, smiling up at him when he cupped her face and stared intently at her. "You look good, Amanda. You look happy. Are you?"

She stared at him for a moment before nodding. "I am. I met someone and he's a good guy."

"Good. You deserve a good guy," Jamie said. "You gonna marry him?"

"Honestly, I've kind of fucked it up at the moment, but I'm going to try to fix it tonight. If it isn't too late."

"It won't be," Jamie said. "If he's a smart guy, he'll know how amazing you are."

He bent his head and kissed her on the forehead. "Take care, Amanda."

"You too, Jamie. Thanks for coming to see me."

He nodded and hugged her again before leaving the salon. She sat down at her station and stared at her reflection in the mirror. She loved Max and even if it was too late for them, she was going to tell him. She had to.

Max hurried down the sidewalk toward the salon. It was almost noon and he wanted to catch Amanda before she left for lunch. He grabbed the door handle to the salon and peered in through the window before freezing in place.

Amanda was standing in the middle of the salon and as he watched, she hugged the man standing next to her. Max had only seen his face once on an iPad screen, but he knew immediately who he was and anger flooded through him. Her asshole ex was back in town and Amanda was hugging him.

A second wave of bitter anger rushed through him when Jamie cupped her face and kissed her forehead. Amanda smiled sweetly at him and Max dropped the handle like it was on fire before turning and striding rapidly away.

"Hey, Luce?"

Lucy turned and smiled at Jason. "Hi, honey. What's up?"

"You need to talk to Max."

"What? Why?"

Jason leaned against the doorway. "He's in his office and he is pissed about something."

"Pissed about work?"

"I don't think so," Jason said. "I asked him what was wrong, and he shouted that he was fine and asked me to leave. If I weren't his boss, I'm pretty sure he would have told me to get the fuck out of his office."

Lucy stood and hurried toward the doorway of her office. "I'll talk to him. Thanks, honey."

Jason rubbed her belly as she slipped by him and she paused and laughed before saying in a low voice, "If you keep rubbing my belly every time you're near me, people are going to figure it out, Jason."

He shrugged and gave her an adorable grin. "The ultra-sound went fine this morning. I think we should start telling our co-workers."

"Let's tell our families first," Lucy said before giving him a quick peck on the cheek. "We'll tell Jerry and everyone else next week, okay?"

"Deal," Jason said. He gave her belly one last stroke before heading to his office. Lucy walked to Max's office and knocked on the door.

"Not now," Max snarled.

She opened the door and stepped into the room as Max whirled around. "I said not -"

He paused and blew his breath out. "This isn't a good time, Lucy."

"Tell me what's wrong."

"There's nothing wrong," he said. "I'm frustrated with work right now."

"This doesn't feel like a work thing," Lucy said.

He glared at her before staring out the window and muttering, "It is."

"Max," Lucy said, "please tell me what's wrong."

He didn't reply and she walked across the room and touched his back. "Maybe I can help."

"When did Amanda get back together with her dirtbag ex?"

"What?" Lucy blinked at him in surprise and Max gave her an impatient look. "When did she get back together with that asshole? Tell me the truth."

"I don't know what you're talking about," Lucy said.

Max snorted angrily before pacing back and forth. "I went to the salon at lunch to see if Amanda wanted to have lunch with me. Her ex was in the salon and they were – were hugging. He kissed her and she smiled at him. I thought she was done with him, thought maybe she was done with the fucking bad boys – what a fool I am."

"I don't know why she was with Jamie but there has to be an explanation for it," Lucy said. "She's done with him."

"Is she?" Max asked. "Or did she only tell us she was? She did that before, didn't she? Told you that she wouldn't let him drag her back into his life, but it wasn't true. She was still seeing him. Maybe she is now. Maybe she's been lying to the both of us for months."

"She isn't," Lucy said. "Honey, she doesn't love Jamie. In fact, I'm pretty sure she's in love with -"

"I don't care!" Max shouted. "If she wants her goddamn bad boy so much, she can have him. I'm done, Lucy. Do you hear me? I'm done."

"I hear you," she said. "But before you freak out, maybe you should talk to Amanda and let her explain. You don't know what you saw for sure. Why don't you take the afternoon off and go talk to her?"

"No," Max said. "I have a lot of work to do and there's no point in talking to her. I'm never going to be the guy she wants me to be."

"Max -"

"Can you go, Lucy? I need to get back to work."

"Okay," Lucy said. She turned and left his office as Max sat in his chair and stared angrily at his computer screen.

She hurried back to her office and grabbed her cell phone. She called Amanda, tapping her finger impatiently on the top of her desk. She didn't know what the hell was going on but if Amanda was back together with that dirtbag Jamie, she would beat the crap out of her – best friend or not.

AMANDA CHECKED THE APPOINTMENT BOOK. THE AFTERNOON was dragging by and she didn't have a single appointment to distract her. She sighed as Angie grinned at her.

"Slow day, huh?"

"Stupidly slow," Amanda replied as her cell phone rang. She hit the answer button. "Hey, Luce? What's up?"

"Are you back together with Jamie?" Lucy said.

"What? No, of course I'm not."

"Then why did Max see you hugging him in the salon today? Amanda, if you're back together with that asshole, I swear to God I will kick your ass."

"I'm not back together with him," Amanda said. "What do you mean Max saw us hugging?"

"He saw you hugging. He's in a horrible mood and when I asked him what was wrong, he said he dropped by the salon at lunch and you were in there hugging Jamie. He said Jamie kissed you!"

"He kissed me on the forehead. Luce, I'm not back together with him. He was here to apologize."

"You can't believe him, Amanda! He's trying to suck you back in and -"

"Is Max still at the office?" Amanda said.

"Yes, and he's pissed as hell."

"I'll be right there." Amanda ended the call before Lucy could reply and ran to the back room to grab her purse. "Angie, I have to go."

"What? Why?" Angie asked.

"I just – I have to go. I don't have any appointments and Bethany will be here at two so you're only alone for an hour or so."

"Okay," Angie said. "Um, I'll see you tomorrow?"

"Yes," Amanda said as she hurried out of the salon.

"MAX?"

Max's head snapped up and he stared at Amanda standing in the doorway of his office. "What are you doing here?"

"Lucy called me. She told me you were upset."

"I'm very busy. You shouldn't have come here," he said.

She shut the door to his office and leaned against it. "We need to talk."

"No, we don't. I know you're back with Jamie and I don't care. We're just friends and if you want to fuck up your life with a loser like him, I can't stop you. I know how much you love your goddamn bad boys."

"I don't love him, Max and I'm not back together with -"

"I don't care!" he repeated before he shoved his chair back and stood. He glared at her. "Do you have any idea how amazing you are, Amanda? Do you have any idea how hard it is to listen to you put yourself down? To try to convince you that you're not the person that all those fucking bad boys told you that you were?"

"I know. I'm sorry. I shouldn't have been putting my own insecurities on you like that and I feel terrible about it. But, Max, I get it now. I know that how I view myself isn't healthy or accurate and I promise you that I'm going to work on it. I'm going to try to see myself the way you do because how you see me is the person that I want to be. All of those horrible guys I dated weren't good for me and I know that. I know that I need someone like you."

"Someone like me," he snorted. "Someone who's nice and boring? How many times have you told me that you want a bad guy? I'm not that guy, Amanda, and I never will be and I'm tired of feeling ashamed that I'm a nice guy. I'm sorry that you're not into nice guys but this is who I am, and I can't change. Not even for you. I wish I could and how fucked up is that? I actually wish I wasn't so nice just so that I could have your love, but I can't be someone I'm not."

"I like you, very much," she said.

"And you know what? It's a shitty thing for you to expect me to… what did you say?"

"I like you, very much. Just as you are."

"Did you – did you just Bridget Jones me?"

She smiled at him. "I did. But in all honesty – it's not exactly an accurate statement of how I feel about you."

"What do you mean?"

"I love you, very much. Just as you are," she said.

His Adam's apple worked convulsively before he said, "You love me."

"Yes. I'm sorry it took me so long to realize it and I know that you're dating Gina now but if you would give me the chance to -"

"I'm not dating Gina," he said.

"You – you went out with her last night," she said.

"I went for drinks with her so I could tell her in person that I was only interested in being friends. Because I'm a nice guy," he replied.

Relief rushed through her and she smiled again. "You are a nice guy, Max. The nicest, sweetest guy I know and it's the second thing I love most about you."

"What's the first?" he said.

"Your filthy mouth and big dick," she said.

He laughed and she walked over to him and touched his arm. "Max, I'm not with Jamie, I swear. I haven't seen or talked to him since that day you told me to kick him out of my life. He showed up at the salon today because he had gone to rehab and gotten sober, and he wanted to apologize to me. That's all it was – an apology for how horribly he had treated me. He told me that all the awful shit he said wasn't true and," she paused and shrugged, "I don't know, maybe I needed to hear from him that I wasn't clingy or a – a bad girl-friend. Or maybe I finally smartened up and realized it on my own but either way – I'm not back together with him. I want to be with you, Max, and not just as friends or as friends with benefits. It's killing me to be apart from you."

"Me too," he said hoarsely.

"So, what do you think? Will you give me a chance?" she said.

He pulled her into his embrace and kissed her. "I love you, Butterfly."

"Just as I am?" she said with a soft smile.

"Just as you are."

EPILOGUE

"**O**h God, my ankles are so swollen."

Lucy examined Amanda's feet before sinking back in her lawn chair. "Yup, they are."

"Thanks," Amanda said with a laugh.

Lucy shrugged. "I feel your pain, honey."

She raised her glass of water and Amanda clinked it with hers before they both took a drink.

"So, have you finished decorating the -"

"Mama!"

Lucy gazed across the lawn at the little boy standing next to the t-ball stand.

"Hi, honey," she said and blew him a kiss.

"Watch me, Mama!" he shouted.

She and Amanda watched as Jason carefully helped the little boy balance the plastic bat on his shoulder. Amanda smiled when he swung and missed, his sturdy body spinning around before he fell on his butt with a thud.

His face screwed up and Jason set him on his feet before dusting off his butt and kissing his cheek. "You're okay, buddy. No need to cry – let's try again."

"Otay, Daddy," the little boy said.

"So, Jason's trying to get Ethan started early in his baseball career, huh?" Amanda said.

Lucy laughed. "He is. Between you and me, I'm not so sure that Ethan's athletic."

"He's only three," Max said as he came out of the house and stood next to Amanda. "It's a scientific fact that you can't tell if a kid is going to be good at sports until they're five."

"Scientific fact, huh?" Lucy said.

Max nodded. "Yes. Very scientific."

He bent and kissed Amanda. "How are you feeling?"

"I'm good," she said. "Stop worrying."

"I'm not worrying," Max said.

Amanda turned to Lucy. "He mapped out the fastest route to the hospital from your new house in case I went into labour during dinner tonight."

Lucy laughed. "You're not due for another two weeks."

"I like to be prepared," Max said. He started toward Jason and Ethan, and Amanda tapped him on the leg.

"Can you help me out of this lawn chair? I've got to pee."

Max grinned cheekily at her before rubbing her large belly. "I told you not to sit in the lawn chair."

"Just help me up, mister," she said with a mock scowl.

He grinned again before hooking his hands in her armpits and lifting her out of the chair. She smoothed her dress down and patted her belly as Lucy snickered. Amanda gave her a tart look. "Why don't you show me how you can get out of your chair, Luce."

Lucy stuck her tongue out at her, and Max laughed. "Want me to help you, Lucy?"

She hesitated before nodding. "Might as well. It's been ten minutes since I peed, so I imagine I'll have to go any moment now."

Max picked her up out of the lawn chair and she tugged her shirt over her own large belly before smiling at him. "Thanks, big guy."

"No problem."

"Mama!" Ethan barreled toward her and latched onto her leg. "I hit the ball."

"Good job, little man!" She smoothed his dark hair back from his face and kissed Jason when he joined them. "You should start the barbeque, honey."

"Sure. Ethan, why don't you show Uncle Max how to hit the ball while Daddy starts cooking?"

"Kay," Ethan said before taking Max's hand.

Jason patted Lucy's belly affectionately as Max elbowed him. "What do you think the odds are of our wives going into labour on the same day?"

"Not going to happen," Lucy said. "I'm not due for three weeks and I can guarantee you I won't be early. Not if she's anything like her brother, anyway."

Jason grinned at Max. "When Amanda is four days overdue and begging you to 'get this kid out of her', I suggest a back rub and a bowl of ice cream."

"Thanks for the tip," Max said as Ethan tugged him toward the t-ball set.

As Jason moved to the barbeque, Lucy took Amanda's hand and squeezed it. "Can you believe you're going to be a mom in two weeks?"

Amanda smiled at her. "Can you believe you're going to be a mom *again* in three weeks?"

Lucy leaned forward and kissed her on the cheek. "We are the luckiest women in the world."

"We really are," Amanda said.

Lucy linked her arm around Amanda's. "Now, let's go into the house before we both wet our pants."

Amanda laughed. "That's an excellent idea."

Keep reading for an excerpt of "Sweet Harmony", Book One
in the Harmony Falls Series

SWEET HARMONY EXCERPT

When the doorbell rang, Kira smoothed down her blonde hair and checked her reflection in the toaster. Not that it really mattered what she looked like. This wasn't a first date for God's sake.

She headed out of the kitchen and down the hallway. Two long windows flanked the front door and she could see one tanned arm and hand through the right one. Her dentist had big hands.

You know what they say about big hands.

She flushed and tossed that errant thought out of her head before opening the door. She smiled at the dark-haired man standing on her front porch.

"Hello, Dr. MacMillan."

"Hello, Ms. Walker," he said.

There was a moment of awkward silence and then she stepped back. "Call me Kira. Please, come in."

He stepped into the house and she shut the door before

squeezing past him. "Would you like something to drink? I have water, iced tea and soda. Or I can make coffee."

"An iced tea would be fine," he said.

As he followed her toward the kitchen, she wondered if he was checking out her ass in her yoga pants. She knew she didn't have a great body. She was on the thin side and she secretly coveted Grace's full curves. She scoffed inwardly. Who was she kidding? Forget Grace's curves, she'd take Addison's very respectable C-cup boobs if given the chance. She was barely a B-cup and her cleavage was thanks to the miracle invention of the century – the push-up bra.

Why she even thought her dentist would check out her ass was ridiculous. It was flat and –

Hey, Kira? Maybe you should stop thinking about your own damn tits and ass and get the man his iced tea.

Dr. MacMillan was hovering in the doorway of the kitchen while she stood blankly next to the fridge and she gave him an embarrassed smile. "Sorry. Have a seat and I'll get that iced tea."

"Thank you," he said.

She poured them both a glass of iced tea and perched on the edge of the chair across from him. He drank some iced tea before saying, "It's good. Thanks."

"I like it a little on the sweet side," she said. "My brother says it's way too sweet and that I'll rot my teeth right out of my head but I, um, I guess that's why I go to see you, right? To keep my teeth from rotting out of my head when I eat too much sweet stuff?"

Kira! Enough!

She shut her mouth with a snap. Fuck, what was wrong with her? Why was she so damn nervous? Sure, Dr. MacMillan was handsome enough, but he wasn't Daniel. She closed her eyes for a moment and conjured up an image of

Daniel. It calmed her a little and she took a deep breath. Daniel's blond hair and dark blue eyes were what she wanted.

Dr. MacMillan's eyes might be blue, but they were so light, they were almost clear. She could see none of the warmth and humour in them that Daniel's gaze had. In fact, her dentist was currently staring at her like she was some new and interesting species of bug he had discovered crawling up his leg.

She cleared her throat. "Sorry, I babble when I'm nervous."

He took another drink of iced tea. "You have a nice home."

"Thank you. It was my childhood home. It belongs to my brother now, but he didn't want to live here. My parents died a few years ago and being in the house brought on too many sad memories for him. I love living here though. It makes me feel closer to my mom and dad, you know?"

She closed her mouth again. Holy shit, she was making the worst first impression ever.

"I'm sorry about your parents." His voice was a low rasp, and the sound of it sent the weirdest shiver down her spine.

"Thank you," she replied. "So, um, Grace said that we could help each other with our problems."

He nodded. "Possibly."

She waited and tried not to sigh with frustration when he didn't say anything else. His silence was beginning to unnerve her. Daniel was chatty and always the life of the party. She could barely get a word in edgewise when she was with him and she loved that. She loved his bold brashness and the way he lit up a room when he walked into it.

Her dentist hardly made an impact. Hell, she'd met him how many times in his office and she had no impression of him at all. He was just a masked guy who came in and checked her teeth at the end of the cleaning.

"So, you need a date for your cousin's wedding?" she asked.

"Yes," he said, "and you need a boyfriend to make Daniel Moore jealous."

There was the slightest hint of derision in his voice and she immediately blushed. It was obvious that he thought she was an idiot.

"You know what? Never mind, Dr. MacMillan." She stood and dumped her iced tea down the sink. "This isn't going to work. I'll show you out now."

She stalked toward the front door. She could hear him behind her, but before she could open the door, he wrapped his long fingers around her wrist. The touch of his skin against hers made another one of those little shivers zip down her spinal cord. She froze and turned to stare up at him.

"I'm sorry," he said. "I'm being an ass."

"Yes, you are."

He sighed and dropped her wrist before raking his hand through his dark hair. "I apologize. Also, if we're going to fake date, you should call me Connor."

"Why are you even here, Connor?" she asked. "It's obvious you think this is a stupid idea."

"It isn't," he said. "I'm just -"

He paused and rubbed at one temple. "What if this doesn't work?"

"What do you mean?"

"What if us fake dating doesn't make Daniel jealous? Will you still go with me to my cousin's wedding? Still pretend to be my girlfriend?"

"Yes," she said.

"What if it does work? Then what? You start dating Daniel and I'm headed to Willington alone."

"Well, your cousin's wedding is in a month, right?"

"Yes."

"We don't have to start fake dating right away. We can give it a couple of weeks and use that time to learn more about each other. It's probably a good idea if we know more than each other's names. It'll be more believable if we know, uh, personal stuff about each other. That leaves only two weeks until your cousin's wedding. I think it'll take more than a couple weeks to make Daniel jealous," she said.

"Do I have your word that you'll attend the wedding with me?" he asked.

"Yes," she said. "I'll be there, no matter what."

Then we have an agreement," Connor said. "You'll pose as my girlfriend at my cousin's wedding, and I'll help you make Daniel seethe with jealousy and realize that you're his soul mate."

She gave him a dirty look. "You don't have to make it sound so juvenile."

He just shrugged and she reached for the front door. "Thank you. I'll get your number from Grace and text you in the next few days about meeting to go over personal stuff."

"There's just one more thing," Connor said.

"What?"

"This." He gripped the back of her neck and pulled her forward. She made a decidedly stupid-sounding squeak when he bent his dark head and pressed his mouth against hers. She stood stock-still with her eyes wide and unblinking, as he slid his other arm around her waist and pulled her against his hard body.

When he sucked on her lower lip, a strange tingle went through her lower body and another small sound escaped her lips. This one, embarrassingly enough, sounded like a moan and she tried to step back. His hand tightened around her neck, holding her completely immobile. When his tongue slid across her upper lip, she heard another of those odd moan-like noises as her eyes drifted shut.

God, he smells so good, she thought bewilderedly as he tilted her head back. He kissed her again, his lips warm and weirdly persuasive, and it took her a minute to realize that she was returning his kiss.

Kira! Stop kissing your dentist!

It was solid advice, but her body was completely and blissfully betraying her. She pressed up against him and put her arms around his neck. He was so tall that it was a real stretch to do it, but she liked the way it forced her breasts against his chest.

His tongue licked the seam of her mouth. Her head whirling and her pussy suddenly throbbing, she parted her lips. He slid his tongue between them and tasted her with slow, long licks that made Kira shudder with pleasure. He tasted sweet like the iced tea he had been drinking. When she pushed her tongue into his mouth with a decided lack of finesse, he slid his fingers into her hair and tugged her back.

"Slow," he whispered.

She blushed fiercely. For roughly a nanosecond, she thought about telling him to stop, but then his warm mouth returned to hers and he was urging her tongue back into his mouth with slow licks of his. She slowed down and mimicked the slow strokes of his tongue.

He groaned quietly. Other than his low whisper it was the first sound he had made since kissing her. It flamed the lust in her belly even higher. She had a feeling that the icy Dr. Connor MacMillan never lost control. The idea that kissing her could make that control slip, even a little, was deliciously intoxicating.

She arched her back and rubbed her abdomen against the hardness pressing into it. He was hard. He was hard for her, and that sent another flickering flame of excitement through her nerve endings. She rubbed her small breasts against him and wondered what she could do to get him to touch them. Her nipples were almost painfully hard and poking against her bra. A sudden vision of Connor sucking on them brought on a gush of liquid that soaked the crotch of her panties.

He pulled away abruptly, and she would have fallen in a boneless heap to the floor if he hadn't steadied her. She stared dumbly at him before reaching up and touching her trembling, swollen lips.

"Why-why did you do that?" she whispered.

"If we're posing as boyfriend and girlfriend, it's going to require some physical touching and kissing," he said.

She felt like she'd been through the wringer, but he wasn't even out of breath. If it hadn't been for the way his dick still strained at the front of his pants, she would have thought he was completely unaffected by the kiss between them.

"O-only when we're around other people." She couldn't seem to stop stuttering or touching her swollen mouth.

He gave her an impatient look. "It won't look very realistic if we kiss each other like it's the first time we've ever kissed. And I wanted to see if we had chemistry."

"Do we?" she asked like an idiot.

A brief smile crossed his face and it sent a weird little tingle down the base of her spine. "Yes. I think so, anyway."

She didn't reply and he patted her on the shoulder like she was his sister. "That's a good thing, Kira. It will make it appear more real."

"Uh, right," she said.

He studied her. "How many men have you kissed before?"

"Why?"

"You're not," he paused, "great at kissing."

Her face was so red she was nearly sweating, and she gave him a furious look. "That's a really rude thing to say."

"No, just honest. We'll need to practice some more."

She wanted to tell him to take his idea of practice kissing and stuff it up his piehole, but strangely the thought of kissing him again wasn't entirely unpleasant. Besides, as much as it was a blow to her ego, he probably had a point. She'd kissed two men before him and neither of them had provoked the type of reaction that her dentist's kiss did.

He opened the front door and asked, "What time do you work tomorrow?"

"Uh, I need to be at the office by nine."

"I'll stop by at eight and we'll practice." He left, shutting the door quietly behind him, and she sank against the wall, her fingers still tracing her lower lip. What the hell just happened?

ABOUT THE AUTHOR

Elizabeth Kelly was born and raised in Ontario, Canada. She moved west as a teenager and now lives in Alberta with her husband and a menagerie of pets. She firmly believes that a person can survive solely on sushi and coffee, and only her husband's mad cooking skills prevents her from proving that theory.

For more information about Elizabeth, check out her website at

www.elizabethkelly.ca

facebook.com/EKellyBooks

twitter.com/ElizabethKBooks

instagram.com/elizabethkelly_author

amazon.com/Elizabeth-Kelly/e/B00EOHZ0MS

bookbub.com/authors/elizabeth-kelly

ALSO BY ELIZABETH KELLY

Tempted Series

Tempted

Twice Tempted

Forever Tempted

Breathless

Tempted Trilogy (Books 1-3)

Red Moon Series

Red Moon

Red Moon Rising

Dark Moon

Alpha Moon

Pale Moon

The Recruit Series

The Recruit (Book One)

The Recruit (Book Two)

The Recruit (Book Three)

The Recruit (Book Four)

The Recruit (Book Five)

The Shifters Series

Willow and the Wolf (Book One)

Ava and the Bear (Book Two)

Katarina and the Bird (Book Three)

Porter's Mate (Book Four)

Bria and the Tiger (Book Five)

Rosalie Undone (Book Six)

The Dragon's Mate (Book Seven)

Rise of the Jaguar (Book Eight)

The Draax Series

Reign (Book One)

Rule (Book Two)

Rebel (Book Three)

Harmony Falls Series

Sweet Harmony (Book One)

Perfect Harmony (Book Two)

Forbidden Harmony (Book Three)

Redeeming Harmony (Book Four)

Individual Books

The Necessary Engagement

Amelia's Touch

The Rancher's Daughter

Healing Gabriel

The Contract

A Home for Lily

Saving Charlotte

Shameless

The Fairy Tales Collection

Broken

An Unlikely Seduction

Holiday Romance

The Christmas Wife

The Christmas Rescue

The Christmas Nanny

The Christmas Boss

Sordid Games